SPRING AT THE CORNISH GARDEN CAFÉ

THE CORNISH GARDEN CAFÉ
BOOK ONE

RACHEL GRIFFITHS

COSY COTTAGE BOOKS

Cover Art by Daniela Colleo of StunningBookCovers. com

Copyright © by Rachel A.Griffiths 2025

All rights reserved. This book or any portion thereof may not be reproduced or used in any manner whatsoever without the express written permission of the author, except for the use of brief quotations in a book review.

❦ Created with Vellum

*To all who have loved and lost,
whose hearts carry both love and grief.
I hope this story brings some comfort
and reminds you that even in loss,
love endures.*

CONTENTS

Spring at the Cornish Garden Café   7

1. Ellie Cordwell   9
2. Jasper Holmes   15
3. Ellie   24
4. Pearl Draper   33
5. Ellie   37
6. Pearl   40
7. Jasper   48
8. Ellie   52
9. Pearl   56
10. Jasper   62
11. Ellie   71
12. Ellie   81
13. Jasper   91
14. Ellie   100
15. Jasper   104
16. Ellie   113
17. Jasper   123
18. Ellie   135
19. Jasper   143
20. Ellie   152
21. Ellie   161
22. Jasper   165
23. Ellie   173
24. Pearl   177
25. Ellie   181
26. Jasper   186
27. Ellie   195
28. Jasper   198
29. Jasper   201
30. Ellie   203

31. Jasper	206
Epilogue - Ellie	211
Dear Reader,	217
Acknowledgments	219
About the Author	221
Also by Rachel Griffiths...	223

SPRING AT THE CORNISH GARDEN CAFÉ

Come to Cornwall and spend some time at the charming Cornish Garden Café. Surrounded by a beautiful, peaceful garden, the café is a haven at any time of the year. Breathe in the clean sea air, listen to the waves crashing against the shore and relax while you sip a refreshing drink and enjoy a tasty bite to eat...

Ellie Cordwell seeks refuge with her grandmother, Pearl, in Cornwall after a breakup and the failure of her acting career. Ellie is burnt out and in need of rest and recuperation before she can figure out what comes next.

Successful entrepreneur, Jasper Holmes, is busy with work and raising his two young children. He's gone through his fair share of heartbreak and has made a vow to stay single until his children are grown. In fact, he can't get his head around the thought of ever dating again.

Not one to be complacent, Ellie rolls up her sleeves and helps her grandmother out at the café, in its stunning location near the beach. It's very different to her life in London and she's surprised to find herself enjoying being back in the village she once called home.

Jasper finds new arrival Ellie as refreshing as the sea air, but friendship is all he's interested in. His heart is fragile, and he can't risk it again because he has to be strong for his children.

As the spring flowers bloom and the air grows warmer with the promise of summer, something blossoms between Ellie and Jasper. Will they allow their feelings to grow like the flowers in the garden or will they part ways as the summer waves roll in?

1
ELLIE CORDWELL

There will be a time in everyone's life when they reach a crossroads, and for Ellie Cordwell, it happened during an audition for a play.

'OK then, Ms Cordwell, we'd like you to perform your tap solo.' The casting director looked up from her clipboard. On the stage, bathed in the full glare of the spotlight, Ellie tried not to tremble. In her black running tights (that had never seen a run), her black spandex vest top (that had also never seen a run) and her black lace-up pumps (purchased several months ago specifically for auditions), she had felt sophisticated and professional leaving the house, but now... not so much. The four people sitting in the third row of red velvet seats were staring at her, practically holding their breath in anticipation. She was here to be judged on her ability, her talent, and — there was no denying this — her looks.

A hush had fallen over the theatre (only a skeleton crew was present as it was a chilly Friday morning in February and only the brave had ventured out) and Ellie felt the pressure mounting.

'A tap what?' Her voice squeaked at the end of *what*, and she winced at how weak it sounded. Weakness was not a good look during an audition.

'Your tap solo, Ms Cordwell. There's a scene in the play that requires the female lead to perform a tap solo and…' The casting director looked down at her clipboard again. Her green hair fell into her face, so she tucked it behind her ears. 'Your agent was definitely informed that the ability to tap dance was desirable. She told you about this, surely?'

Ellie gulped. *Her agent.* Signing with the renowned Ramona Renoir, famous for her ferocity in defending her clients and her unwavering ability to negotiate the very best roles for them, had not really worked out well for Ellie. Her boyfriend's parents were good friends with Ramona and had initiated the introduction a few years after Ellie had graduated. Ramona had been polite towards Ellie during that first meeting but had not offered to sign her. This had set a precedent for their following meetings, each one engineered by Barnaby's parents. Mr and Mrs Beauchamp had been keen to see their son's partner enjoy a successful acting career, which would also have benefitted him. Their only son was the apple of their eyes, and they wanted the very best for him. In fact, they would do *whatever* was required to facilitate it. Ellie suspected the reason Ramona had eventually signed her was not because the agent had eventually *seen the light* but because of some bribery on the Beauchamps' part.

'Ms Cordwell! It's quite a simple question.' This time, the casting director's tone was sharp. She sat forwards, fixing Ellie with a steel-blue glare that would turn anxious actors to quivering wrecks. *Just like now!* 'Did your agent tell you that you would be required to tap dance for the audition?'

Ellie inhaled slowly, flicked her long black hair, and gave herself an inward shake.

'She did.' The lie rolled off her tongue. 'However, I have … uh… forgotten my tap shoes.'

'Hmmmm.' The casting director looked to the people on either side of her as if to check that they must also think Ellie was an idiot. But then she shrugged. 'That's fine. Just do what you can.'

'Sure.' Ellie sucked in another deep breath.

Tap dance?

She had never tap-danced in her life, but it couldn't be that hard, surely? She'd done some dance as a young child, but that had been a long time ago. Accepting that she wasn't the most coordinated of people, she had decided to focus on auditioning for more serious roles. Her dream had been to appear on an ITV or Netflix drama, to have the starring role in a psychological thriller that would have reviewers raving about her and casting directors flocking to sign this *amazing new talent*. However, so far, that hadn't happened, although she was aware that some of Ramona's clients had acquired such roles — including Ramona's daughter.

'Do you have some music I could dance to?' Ellie asked, wringing her hands.

'Nope. Just go for it.' The casting director sat back and steepled her fingers under her chin.

Ellie's cheeks started burning. She'd always known that showbiz was not an easy career path to follow, but hadn't thought people would be so bloody cold. She'd imagined more *lovey-dovey* behaviour and thought she'd find dear friends and employers who would nurture her, encourage her to reach for the stars. That, however, did not seem likely to happen. Not that she didn't think people could forge warm relationships in the showbiz world, but so far — she'd graduated seven years ago — it had not happened for her.

'OK then.' She cleared her throat. 'Here goes.'

She started swaying her hips from side to side to loosen them and then tried to imagine music was playing. As she tapped her left foot, a memory struck her from years ago when she'd watched *Singin' in the Rain* with her gran. There had been a scene in that when the three characters had sung *Good Morning* as they danced around. She started to hum the song softly, then she began to move.

Soon, she found herself getting into the rhythm.

Yes!

She could absolutely do this. It wasn't that challenging and...

Wow!

It was quite energetic, though.

Breathe, Ellie! Breathe!

Somehow, the tune in her head morphed into Gloria Estefan's *Rhythm is Gonna Get You*. She shook her hips, then threw in some jazz hands as she twisted and turned on the stage, skipping from one side to the other.

And now for a...

Shimmy... Shimmy! Shimmy! Shimmy!

Oh yeah, you're really doing it, Ellie! You must look soooo good!

She glanced at her audience and saw that their eyes were wide and one of them had got his phone out. The fact that he was filming her meant she must be blowing their minds with her excellent performance. This would be the audition to end all auditions. She'd end up on Broadway and win awards and…

She started to can-can as the song progressed in her head, kicking her legs high, waving her hands at her sides.

And ... One! Two! Three!

Kick! Kick! Kick!

A bead of sweat trickled down her forehead, made its way down the side of her face, then plopped onto her shoulder.

Kick! Kick! Kick!

Almost there…

Kick!

And what followed seemed to happen in slow motion.

Her left leg went up.

Came down.

Went up again…

Her pump shot off… Hurtled through the air…

The faces of her audience changed from awe to fear as they watched her pump hit the casting director smack in the middle of her smug face.

Ellie froze mid kick.

Silence settled over the scene.

The casting director recoiled in her seat, a scream escaping as blood gushed down her face.

What followed was utter chaos as the team shuffled out of the row without so much as a backwards glance. Ellie was left alone on the stage. Breathless. Sweating. Wondering what to do next.

She waited for a few moments, thinking someone would come back and speak to her, but no one did. Instead, her phone pinged from her bag at the side of the stage, so she got it out and peered at the screen.

It was a message from Ramona.

> **Ellie,**
> **You didn't get the role. *Again*.**
> **Our time together has come to an end.**
> **Wishing you luck in your future endeavours.**
> **Best,**
> **Ramona**

Ellie read the brief but very clear message three times, then stuffed her phone back in her bag, pulled on her coat and limped off the stage. She considered trying to locate her pump but decided not to bother, as it would probably be covered in the casting director's blood.

It seemed her career in acting was well and truly over, and she had no idea what she was going to do next. All she wanted was a hot bath, a mug of tea, and a nap.

Her gran had always told her that everything happens for a reason. Right now, Ellie couldn't possibly conceive of a universe where, in this instance, her gran would be right.

2
JASPER HOLMES

*J*asper Holmes unlocked his front door and went inside, keen to warm up after doing the school run on the chilly February morning. The sound of claws on wooden floorboards almost made him groan because he knew it meant he had to head back out into the cold again. But then he couldn't be annoyed with his best friend in the whole world, now, could he?

'Hello, Wiggy. Decided to get up, have you?' He crouched down as his chocolate Labrador trotted towards him, tail wagging so hard that his entire bottom moved with it.

Wiggy, possibly the daftest dog in the world, showered Jasper with doggy kisses. Jasper chuckled despite the fact that Wiggy's breath smelt of the tuna and chicken food he'd consumed for breakfast.

Once Wiggy had finished his enthusiastic greeting, Jasper led the way to the kitchen, where he filled a glass with water from the tap and drank it down. His eyes were drawn to the kitchen window that overlooked the rear garden with its breathtaking view of the coastline. The housing development where Jasper lived with his two children, seven-year-old Mabel, and five-year-old Alfie, had a view that Jasper knew he sometimes failed to appreciate fully. Of course, there were reasons he failed to appreciate it, reasons he suspected most people would understand. Even though he had so much to be grateful for, he often felt like he was living a half-life. Not that he didn't adore his children, because he did with his whole heart, but he no longer felt complete. Jasper would do anything for his children, but the one thing he couldn't do was give them their mum back. And this was a source of utter heartbreak for him, because raising two young children without their mum present was incredibly challenging. Jasper loved being a dad, absolutely loved it, but he wished his children had their mum with her loving heart, her beautiful smile, her warm hugs, and the laugh that lit up every room she entered.

Jasper and his wife, Kimberley, had chosen the house *together*. They had decided to move to the small Cornish fishing village *together*. And when they had done so four years ago, their hearts had been filled with joy about the life they were about to embark upon with their two children. They had spent years saving, scrimping, doing without expensive nights out and other luxuries, in order to save enough so they could buy their dream house in their dream location. The problem with dreams was that people could spend a long time nurturing them, a long time believing that those dreams were exactly what they wanted, and during that time they could well be ignoring what they already had. Jasper knew now that he had once had *everything*. Everything he had wanted. Everything he had needed. But he had wished away precious times when, in fact, he should have been treasuring them. How could Jasper move on, how could he embrace life fully, when he felt so guilty for taking for granted the time he'd had with his beautiful wife? He had outlived her, had held her in his arms as the life flowed slowly from her, and he would have given anything, anything at all, to have taken her place. His wife had been his entire world; the reason he did everything from getting up in the morning to working hard, to putting out the bins and to learning how to make nutritious new meals. Without Kimberley around, none of it felt like he was making a difference.

'Come on Wiggy,' he said. 'Let's get you out for your morning walk, then we can come home, make coffee and I'll get to work.'

Thank goodness for his job, he thought, as he strapped the dog into his harness and clipped on the lead. He grabbed a roll of poo bags from the cupboard in the hallway and tucked them into his pocket. His job gave him a purpose when his children were at school. As a tech entrepreneur helping businesses thrive, his work fully absorbed his mind, leaving no time for dwelling, grieving, or pain. In fact, some days it meant that the hours flew by and he would look at the clock in surprise. As a result, he had long ago come to the conclusion that it would be best for him if he set an alarm to remind him it would soon be time to collect the children from school. He ended up setting two alarms, one to remind him to stretch his legs, and one to remind him to get ready to collect the children.

Wiggy often declined to join him on the morning school run, preferring to stay in his comfortable bed near the log burner in the lounge, but he tended to enjoy an afternoon stroll to the school to collect the children. And in typical rescue dog fashion, Wiggy adored his humans. The dog was four, but he had only been with Jasper for two years. Jasper had decided to adopt a rescue dog after seeing yet another heart-breaking charity advert on television. He'd been aware there was a rescue centre not far from the village, based at one of the local farms, but he hadn't ever been there before. His wife had always talked of adopting a rescue dog, but it was one of those things they'd never got around to because they'd been so busy saving and so focused on moving. For Jasper, this was another reason he wished he'd done it sooner. Kimberley would have loved Wiggy. Jasper could imagine them together, snuggling, walking, and playing. He could imagine the dog following his wife around the house, tripping her up as she made scrambled eggs, sniffing at her feet when she returned from work, food shopping or taking the children to school. Jasper knew Wiggy would have been his wife's shadow, and that was something that broke his heart. And yet, it was as if Wiggy had come into Jasper's life at the right time, at the point when he was destined to be adopted. At the point when Jasper needed to be saved.

Jasper had been struggling for a year after losing his wife. He'd been going through the motions, getting up in the morning, feeding the children, taking them to school, coming home, turning on his computer and working. He'd lost a lot of weight as he grieved, and it was only when his stomach rumbled or when he felt faint from low blood sugar that he actually remembered to eat. One day, he'd been sitting on the sofa sipping a mug of coffee, when the advert for one of the dog rescue charities had come on TV. He saw the faces of the abandoned and mistreated dogs looking for new families. It had triggered something inside him that had made him decide, on the spot, that he needed to adopt a dog. Following contact with the rescue centre, he went there the next day. He'd gone without the children, of course, because if he'd taken them along, he'd have come home with ten dogs. He also knew the children would have wanted to bring the dog home immediately, and that wasn't possible because there were procedures in place to protect the animals and the prospective owners. And so Jasper had gone through the process of filling in the application form, meeting the dogs available and having a home check. The latter had involved a very nice lady visiting his home, checking out the garden and asking some questions. During the process, as soon as Jasper met Wiggy, he had fallen in love with the dog and known that he wanted to bring him home. There was something in Wiggy's eyes that echoed something Jasper felt in his heart, and he knew the Lab was the right dog for his family. Once the children and Wiggy had met and it was clear that all involved were happy with the decision, Wiggy came home and settled into his new life. Jasper would not have it any other way now because the dog had brought love, loyalty, laughter, snuggles, and the comfort and security that Jasper had been craving. The best part about this for Jasper, though, was knowing he had provided the same for Wiggy. He knew this because of the way Wiggy followed him around, the way he wagged his tail so hard his entire body swayed, and also because of how well Wiggy had settled into his new life. It was like Wiggy had always been a part of their family and Jasper couldn't imagine life without him.

Now, Jasper let them out of the front door and pulled it shut behind him. They set off along the pavement towards the end of the development and through the gate that led to the coastal path. The proximity to the beach and the coastal path were some of the things that had attracted him and

Kimberley to the location in South Cornwall. What better place to live and raise two children than somewhere so close to the sea? Being able to get up every day and breathe in the fresh sea air, to head to the coastal path and drink in the gorgeous views of the Cornish coast, to stroll down to the beach and paddle in the clear waters of the sea were all reasons enough to spend the extra money required to secure the incredible four-bedroom property.

As they walked, Wiggy wagged his tail and raised his nose into the air, making Jasper laugh. He never tired of wondering what the dog could smell. Was it the salt of the ocean? The fish beneath the surface? The birds that soared and swooped above the water? Did he smell the small animals that nested in the grass on the sides of the coastal path, beneath the earth, or in the fields that spread inland? Did he smell the fuel of an ocean liner or a fishing boat, or even someone's breakfast bacon frying in a pan? Jasper suspected it was a combination of all these things and he almost envied Wiggy's ability to enjoy all these scents. *Almost,* because he knew it would send him into sensory overdrive.

Jasper breathed in deeply and exhaled fully, filling his lungs and then forcing out the air as he envisioned himself being cleansed from within. He knew that being able to control his breathing was important. It helped him feel in control of himself and of the anxiety. Of course, it didn't always work, because sometimes the anxiety rose like a tidal wave that threatened to drown him. It was usually worse in the small hours of the morning, in the time between darkness and dawn, before the birds began to sing, and when the house lay quiet. At those times, he felt more alone than ever. His heart would race in his chest and sometimes he would feel like he couldn't swallow. He had found that the best thing to do was get up and drink a glass of water, wash his face with freezing cold water from the tap, and move his body. He had practised mindfulness for years, but since he had lost his wife, he had become reliant upon it to remain sane. The panic would pass, as it always did, and he would feel calm once more. Not free from pain, not free from grief, not free from being aware of how his life had changed, but knowing that the panic, the anxiety and the all-consuming loneliness would pass. Dawn would come, bringing with it sweet bird song, the brightening of the sky, and a new day in which he would strive to be the best father possible, the best dog dad possible, and the best form of himself that he could be.

The anger though... He didn't know if he would ever fully master the anger because the anger kept him going, the anger was perhaps the hardest thing of all to become master of. How could he not be angry when his wife had been stolen away from him by someone choosing to be careless, choosing to live dangerously, choosing to ignore the fact that they could cause harm to others and steal away the woman who was one little family's entire world?

When the coastal path opened out, Jasper unclipped Wiggy's lead from his harness and let the dog jog on ahead. Wiggy never went far; he always kept Jasper in his sights, but he liked to explore a little without the restriction of the lead. Jasper never let Wiggy off on the areas of the path where it wasn't safe, when there were other people around, or other dogs, unless he had checked the dogs were sociable. But with it being a chilly February morning, it seemed the perfect time for Wiggy to have a little freedom to stretch his legs.

Jasper breathed in deeply again and exhaled, tasting the salt on his lips from the wind. This time of year, the scenery was rugged and on the path ahead, tufts of sharp grass grew out from between the rocks, but he knew that a variety of colourful plants would soon awaken after the winter. Despite his grief, Jasper sometimes felt like he was emerging from the darkness, albeit slowly and not in a linear fashion. There were moments when he felt as if the sunlight could warm him enough that he might live fully again, but these moments were far apart. Perhaps he would be stuck in an eternal spring, where he occasionally emerged from the winter of grief, but never enough to move into summer.

Jasper laughed out loud. His erratic mind sometimes alarmed, sometimes amused him with its frantic search for solutions. It was like his brain was still trying to make sense of what had happened and to find a way to process it, but perhaps the easiest way of dealing with the pain of grief was denial. It was easy to deny what had happened and sometimes he could do this, but then reality was impossible to escape and every time he returned home, it was clear as day that his wife was gone.

'Wiggy!' he called, and the dog stopped walking. 'Sit!'

Jasper caught up with the dog and gave his ears a rub, then he clipped the lead to his harness. 'I'm thinking we should head on home now and get a warm drink and a snack before I get on with some work. How does that sound to you?'

Wiggy gave a little bark and swept his long furry tail in wide arcs that let Jasper know his suggestion had Wiggy's approval. They turned around and retraced their steps, while the cold February winds whisked grey clouds across the sky like ships across the sea, and seagulls screeched as they swooped down to the water's surface. The water that was constantly moving, the tide caught in a perpetual ebb and flow, much like his grief.

Whatever happened in Jasper's life, he knew that the world would go on. Human beings were only present for a very brief time, and so it was important that they strove to make the most of that time. Jasper's wife had lived that way, and he knew it was her wish for him and their children.

Somehow, Jasper had to be OK with that.

Somehow, Jasper had to keep on keeping on…

3
ELLIE

*E*llie arrived back at Barnaby's parents' North London home with a damp left foot and an ache in her right bum cheek that made her think she might have pulled something doing her high kicks. A bath and a mug of tea were definitely in order to soothe her after the ordeal she'd been through.

As she searched in her bag for the house key, a terrible thought hit her.

Barnaby's parents would be so disappointed in her. They would probably not want their son to continue his relationship with her because who wanted their child involved with a failure? If she had children one day, she wouldn't want them to be in love with someone with no job and no prospects. Perhaps she could avoid telling them about the audition and being let go by Ramona and instead announce her desire to marry and be a stay-at-home parent. Or was that home maker? Who knew what the correct term was these days? Language kept developing and Ellie often found herself putting her foot in it with her boyfriend who was a stickler for being politically correct. According to Barnaby, a fisherman was no longer that but a fisher. Blonde hair was now blond, regardless of gender. Ellie struggled to absorb it all on a daily basis. And now, this crisis … Hitting the casting director in the face with your footwear was unacceptable, especially when you broke said person's nose. Or so she'd read in the *Actors R Us* WhatsApp group she was in, where she had not been named but where her mishap had become the day's delicious gossip. Her so-called friends had commented with delight, their emojis expressing shock and horror, but their words expressing so much more. How they would hate to be the centre of such gossip and yet, despite their daily mantras like *Be Kind, You Never Know What Someone's Going Through*, they really did enjoy hearing about things going wrong for someone else. Like vultures, they had picked over the bones of her audition and filled their bellies with her misfortune.

Ellie finally located her key and slid it into the lock, then pushed the door open. The grand hallway spread out before her, the chandelier sparkling, the tiled floor polished, the scent of lilies and freesias filling the air. There was a faint hint of last night's chicken in a creamy white wine sauce that they had eaten with tender-stem broccoli and baby carrots. Ellie's stomach growled, reminding her she hadn't eaten that day because of nerves and a desire to keep her stomach flat for the audition. There was nothing worse than being told she might have got the part *if she'd been twenty pounds lighter* or *not quite so big-boned*, as one casting director had put it. Political correctness rarely reached the shady netherworld of the casting couch, and that was, apparently, perfectly fine amongst actors and directors. If you didn't look right for a part, then you could be told so in no uncertain terms. As Ellie had been forced to accept many times.

And yet, she had not succumbed to the fad diets she'd seen her fellow actors endure — like the one that involved drinking water infused with maple syrup and lemon juice while starving oneself for days. She'd also found she couldn't cope with the low-carb diet of eating lots of fatty foods and red meat. Her stomach had been desperate for some fibre after three days, her bowel rather ... bunged... and she'd decided dieting wasn't for her. There were curvy actors out there who did perfectly well, and she aspired to be one of them, to fly the flag for women with boobs and bums everywhere. Oh, to be coveted for magazine covers where she'd embrace her curves and encourage others to do the same because life was for living and enjoying and surely food was part of that? Not that she thought she was greedy, no, but she liked food. Even when she'd been at her thinnest, she'd still had hips and a rounded bottom, both down to genetics that would never change.

And so... Ellie had not forced herself to fit someone else's version of perfection, and now, partly because of that, she had lost her agent and the chance of future auditions. She sagged inwardly for a moment as the full brutality of the situation hit her. *What an awful mess.*

Her stomach growled again, bringing her back to the moment. There was nothing she could do to change what had happened. Everything would (maybe, though she doubted it) seem better in the morning. For now, she needed to eat, soak in a fragrant bubble bath, and drink lots and lots of tea.

Dropping her bag on the bottom of the stairs, she removed her one remaining pump then headed through to the kitchen, already wondering what she would find in the fridge to put in a sandwich.

'Oh!' She jumped when she found Barnaby sitting at the kitchen island. 'I didn't know you'd be home.'

He looked up from his phone as if surprised to see her, too. His eyes slid over her from top to toe in the way that had once made her feel like he was trying to seduce her, but now made her feel like he was assessing her for a role. Assessing her and finding her wanting, that was.

'I thought you were going out today?' Ellie phrased the comment as a question.

'I am and will be... soon. But...' He pushed his floppy ginger hair back from his freckled forehead and sighed. 'I think we need to talk, Ellie.'

Uh oh ...

It was never a good sign when Barnaby said they needed to talk.

'Look ... I'm guessing you've heard.' Ramona's mobile was likely red hot since *#tapdancenosegate*, and someone would have delighted in letting Barnaby know what a failure his girlfriend was. 'Barnaby ... I-I gave it my best at the audition but—'

Barnaby stood up, held up a hand and shook his head. 'No, Ellie! Let me speak first.'

'Oh. OK.' She placed her hands on the surface of the kitchen island and leant against it for support, aware that something was going on here that she would not like. She gazed at Barnaby, watching how his eyes flickered from side to side like he was trying to calculate the square route of something. They'd been together for six years, living together for four — albeit in his parents' home. Ellie thought that *should* mean that they knew each other well, that they were comfortable with each other, but sadly, it wasn't the case. If anything, the longer they were together, the more Ellie felt like Barnaby was a stranger. In the early days of their relationship, she'd believed their passion and adoration would carry them through the years and that they'd always be happy, always be close. But with each passing year, the passion had waned, the emotional intimacy too. Some days, she wondered if she knew Barnaby at all because he seemed like a total stranger, even though they shared a room and a bed, even though she had seen him grow from a man in his early twenties to one who was almost thirty. Surely that should equal closeness, but instead, all she felt, quite often, was very lonely. She'd read that feeling lonely in a relationship was a sign that you needed to put some work in and so she'd tried that, but Barnaby seemed disinterested. He'd accused her of being needy and demanding and told her to relax. She was, she knew, scared to push him too hard in case he turned around and told her he didn't want to be with her anymore and she would have to start over. Even if staying with Barnaby and his parents didn't necessarily equate to happiness, she'd clung to it, paying them most of her bar job salary as rent. The bar job that was meant to be temporary until she scored an acting role, but had turned out to be her only source of income.

'The thing is, Ellie.' Barnaby was frowning now, his pale brows meeting above his long thin nose with its a pointy tip, just like his mother's. During cold weather, the tip turned bright pink and she'd initially found it cute. Found *him* cute. Handsome? To a degree. Hunky? Not really. But she had been attracted to him with his slim physique and pale blue eyes, as well as to his confidence. Time had taught her, though, that his confidence bordering on arrogance came with being certain of his place in the world and of a future that wouldn't involve financial hardship. Barnaby's parents would always have his back and on top of that, he had a trust fund that he'd be able to access when he turned thirty. Barnaby would want for nothing. It wasn't his financial security, however, that had attracted Ellie to him. She'd liked him in the early days of their dating, had found him funny and sweet. They'd seemed to fit and so when she'd met his parents she'd been somewhat overwhelmed by their wealth and status, had worried about not fitting in with them and wanted to run. But Barnaby had told her he loved her and that his parents would too. Somehow, she'd ended up stuck in a cycle of trying to prove herself to the three of them like some prize race horse that they smiled at and patted but one day expected to sell.

'Yes, Barnaby?'

He held up a hand; the palm facing her and shook his head as if he'd called out *CUT!* The director he aspired to be evident even now - although, truth be told, he'd yet to direct anything other than a three minute YouTube documentary about being an aspiring director.

'Ellie … I have come to a realisation.'

She gave a small nod, her neck muscles stiff with nerves. *Here we go...*

'I need to meet my potential and I cannot do it while living at home with my parents. Therefore … I am going travelling for a year.'

'What?'

So he wasn't breaking up with her? Or was he?

'I've booked my flight already, so don't try to stop me. I need to do it for *me*.'

'For *you*? For an entire year? But what about us?'

'You can stay here with Mum and Dad, if you like, and I'll see you when I get back.'

'Barnaby ... You made this decision without speaking to me about it? How's this supposed to make me feel?'

'Your feelings are not my priority. I need to discover who I am before I hit thirty and so I'm going to travel the world and find myself.'

'Oh.' Ellie gripped the marble surface of the island so hard her knuckles turned white. She blinked rapidly. Barnaby was going away. For a year. And he was suggesting that she stayed here and carried on like nothing had changed. Stayed with his parents who didn't seem to like her so much as tolerate her. She'd been hoping to land a job that would allow her to save a deposit for a rental flat, but that seemed impossible now. 'Barnaby ... Can I ask you one thing?'

'As long as it isn't asking me not to go.'

'Did you ... Did you think about asking me to come with you?'

Something flitted across his face, then disappeared. Was it panic? He'd clearly thought this through and knew what he wanted to say to her, but had been expecting more resistance, perhaps?

'This is about me, not you. I know you have things here to do ... like finding a new agent now, it seems, and I need some... space and time.'

'Are we breaking up?' She released the island and slid her arms around her waist, sucked in a shaky breath.

He shrugged. 'Not really. Just *taking a break*.'

'Right. So, basically, Barnaby, you're admitting that you no longer love me.'

A beat of silence fell then stretched out between them. The clock on the wall ticked, filling the silence with a sense of foreboding. The clock made Ellie think of a Macbeth performance she'd once seen, where a giant clock was used as a prop to emphasise Macbeth's thoughts on time.

Ellie met Barnaby's eyes and saw nothing in them. No love. No affection. No compassion.

Whatever happens, happens, and time goes on, regardless.

'There's no need to be that dramatic, Ellie.' Barnaby rolled his eyes, and she hugged herself tighter.

'Well, that's OK, Barnaby, because … because I don't think I love you either.' As she said the words, she knew they were true. It was over. It had been over for some time, but out of fear and habit, they'd stayed together. But now, Barnaby was going away for a year and it was time for Ellie to make a move too.

'Look, Ellie … I'm sure Mum and Dad will let you stay on until you decide what to do or until you find somewhere else.'

'It's OK, Barnaby. I know what I need to do.'

'And what's that?' He cocked a brow, and she forced a smile to her lips.

'I'm going to go home.'

'Home?' His voice wavered as uncertainty took hold. 'What do you mean, *home*? You've lived in London for a decade.'

'But you know what? It never felt like home. I'm going home to Cornwall.'

With that, Ellie stopped hugging herself, pushed back her shoulders and, holding her head high, she marched out of the kitchen, up the stairs and into their shared bedroom. As she started emptying her things out of drawers and piling them on the bed, she felt better than she had done in ages. At last, she had taken back some control over her life and finally, after years of wondering if she wasn't good enough for Barnaby, she now knew she was more than good enough. The fact that he would leave her to go travelling when she'd just lost a part in a play and her agent on the same day showed her exactly how highly he valued her and their relationship. Ellie had tried to make things work with Barnaby, but he had given her the green light to walk away and that was what she was going to do.

But as she looked at the pile of clothes on the bed, a pang of guilt hit her. Her gran had always been her biggest supporter, and she couldn't bear the thought of disappointing her. She had dreamed of Ellie making it big, and now Ellie was going to have to explain that it hadn't worked out. The thought of seeing the disappointment in her gran's eyes was almost worse than anything else. But she would tell her gran the truth; she had no choice. And though it would hurt, Ellie knew that this was the first step toward truly starting over.

She sat on the edge of the bed and sighed. Not everyone's dreams came true, and yet, part of her still wished her shoe story had ended more like Cinderella's—with a happily ever after—rather than the disaster of #shoegate.

4
PEARL DRAPER

Pearl Draper stretched her arms above her head and yawned. She had slept well and felt refreshed, but there was always the temptation to stay warm and cosy in bed and grab a few more winks.

She pushed the duvet back, slid her legs over the edge of the bed, and put her feet in her moccasin style slippers. Reaching for her fluffy red dressing gown, she pulled it over her arms, did up the belt then went to the window. She opened the blinds and gazed out at the beautiful view before her. At just after dawn, the first rays of golden sun warmed the horizon over the sea creating a peachy hue that would soon spread and paint the sky. The houses and cottages of the village seemed to shimmer with the soft glow and it reflected in the windows of the boats that bobbed in the harbour. For the majority of her adult life, since moving in as a new bride of twenty-two, the small, whitewashed cottage in the Cornish village of Porthpenny had been her home. Pearl sent out her daily silent thank you to the universe that she lived in such an incredible place. At seventy-five, she had seen and done a lot, but she never forgot to be grateful for what she had. She knew all too well that life could change in an instant and so she strove to value every single moment and to make the most of every single day.

Downstairs, Pearl padded into her cosy lounge where she opened the curtains before making her way to the kitchen. She filled the kettle and set it on the boiling plate of the Aga. While the water was heating, Pearl opened the back door and gazed out at her small walled garden. The air was icy and refreshing, and she breathed it in, savouring the cold. It was going to be a beautiful day and a flicker of excitement tingled through her at the signs that spring was on the way. The older she got, the more she became convinced that the years passed faster. Sometimes, that sent a shiver of dread through her but she also knew it was important to accept that this was how life worked. No one could live forever, no one could last forever, and that was why she made the most of every day. Along the way, she had lost friends and loved ones, as well as beloved pets. But that was life, and she knew that as much as she might sometimes wish she could stop time and keep everyone she loved around, it was impossible.

She did what she could to take care of herself — she ate well, exercised, drank plenty of water, and she tried to laugh a lot. Laughter was the very best medicine, and she had always admired those who were able to see the humour in situations. A friend of hers had recently been to see the GP for a routine medical. It had included the usual blood pressure test, weight and height measurements, and also blood tests because her friend had been feeling rather tired of late. Pearl's friend had told the GP she suspected she was tired because she was an octogenarian and she was, perhaps, physically slowing down. The GP had asked Pearl's friend a variety of questions, including how many units of alcohol she drank a week. Apparently, when she told the GP all about the range of gins she'd tried recently, he'd asked if she thought she had a problem with alcohol. Pearl's friend replied, 'No I don't have a problem with alcohol at all! In fact, I like it all!' This had led to Pearl and her friend laughing heartily, and when Pearl's friend had offered her a gin and tonic, Pearl had accepted with enthusiasm. And so, they had enjoyed a drink, raised their glasses to living for today and to absent friends, and then they had sat on the woman's decking and watched the sun set over the sea.

Pearl had always been an early riser, firstly as a child, when she had worked on her parents' Cornish dairy farm, and then when she had married and had a young baby. When her daughter, August Draper, had started at the local primary school, Pearl had got a job there and been a teaching assistant for many years. After retiring from her job as a teaching assistant, she had invested her lump sum and some of the money her husband had left her, into the purchase of a small building surrounded by beautiful gardens at the edge of the village. Pearl had always harboured a dream of owning her own café, and the building had seemed the perfect place to renovate and transform. Along with help from some generous locals, she had created a beautiful haven at the centre of the stunning gardens, and that building had become The Garden Café, referred to by tourists as the Cornish Garden Café.

And so, Pearl continued to rise early in order to get to the garden café that was a short walk from her cottage. She didn't mind at all, not even on the cold winter mornings when it was still dark as she walked to work. She especially didn't mind heading out to work on beautiful spring mornings when nature was awakening after its winter sleep, and as for the summer mornings, it was an absolute pleasure to be up and about early before the heat of the day set in.

The kettle began to whistle, so Pearl poured water on a mint tea bag and let it soak while she set about making some breakfast. Once she had eaten, she went upstairs to shower and dress, thinking about what the day ahead would bring, and anticipating the conversations she would have with the local people she had come to know so well. Living in the village where she had been all her adult life, she knew just about everyone. She liked the security and the familiarity of living where she did and knew that she would never want to be anywhere else. Of course she missed her husband, who had passed away twenty years ago, her daughter August, who now lived in Scotland at the side of a loch with her Scottish husband, and her granddaughter, Ellie, who lived in London. But that was life. Pearl believed everyone should be able to go their own way and to live their life the way they chose, as long as they weren't hurting anyone else.

Dressed and ready, she descended the stairs again, pulled on her cosy sheepskin boots and the down filled puffer jacket she had bought in the village charity shop. It was time to get to the garden café, to feed the chickens she kept there for their eggs and to let them out into their run, to feed the wild birds that frequented the beautiful gardens, and then to feed the villagers who would visit the café that day.

Pearl loved her life and felt fortunate to be living it her way.

Every day was a gift indeed.

5
ELLIE

*E*llie's plans had not quite worked out the way she had expected, and it took her several weeks to leave London. For starters, the day after Barnaby had informed Ellie of his plans, he had called a house meeting. His parents had expressed their dismay that (a) he intended to go away for so long and (b) that he was going without Ellie. As much as they usually seemed indifferent towards her, Ellie thought, they seemed to enjoy knowing she was there for Barnaby. Kind of like a babysitter, or the way she constantly tidied up after him, more like an au pair.

Barnaby, however, had explained to his parents, without any desire to spare Ellie's blushes, that he didn't want to be tied down to a life in England without having first experienced the wonders of the world for himself. This had left Ellie somewhat shocked, as growing up, Barnaby had holidayed in exotic and interesting locations, and had never been tied down to his life in England. He had continued to holiday with friends even after he'd started dating Ellie, rarely inviting her along. But now, Barnaby complained that he felt confined and trapped by his relationship with Ellie, and that he needed to escape to discover himself. Diana and Harold Beauchamp had listened. They had initially seemed somewhat shocked, but as their only son told them he felt he was being suffocated by his life, they had decided on the spot that he should indeed go away and find himself. There had been little consideration for Ellie's feelings and she had sat in the kitchen feeling like an outcast. It was very unpleasant, quite humiliating in fact, and something she hoped never to experience again. She would never want to put anyone through the complete cringe fest of being made to feel like she was ruining Barnaby's life — which she had not thought she was doing. According to Barnaby, however, she was not the person he wanted to spend his life with for many reasons. After all, she could never afford to travel the world without worrying about money, debt and how she would manage when she returned to the UK. His parents did not jump to defend her honour at all. It was like she had been there to fulfil a role and they were all disappointed in her performance, so now she would be let go by them in exactly the same way that Ramona had done. The only difference was that Ramona had fired her via text and Barnaby was doing so in the family home in front of his parents. The house meeting had added nothing to Ellie's feelings about what Barnaby had already told her, but it had rubbed salt into the wound. And made her glad that she'd decided to leave.

Mortification complete, she had trudged upstairs to continue her packing, only to be approached by Diana who had asked for a quiet word. Diana had informed Ellie that they were going away on a Caribbean cruise, and therefore their home would be empty for a few weeks. Not wanting to worry about security, they would be very grateful if Ellie would stay there and keep an eye on things. Diana seemed to feel no shame at all in asking and Ellie realised she was not surprised. It made it crystal clear to Ellie that she was nothing more than hired help. She had been hired as Barnaby's girlfriend while it suited them, and now she was being hired as home security.

However, she'd had things that she needed to sort out before she left London — like resigning from her bar job — and so she accepted the role of home security. It would provide the breathing space she needed before she returned to Cornwall. The last thing Ellie wanted was to return to Cornwall before she'd had a chance to take stock of her new situation. Her gran had been more of a mother to her than her biological mother had been and Ellie loved her deeply. Pearl was Ellie's family, her confidante, and the one person she could rely on. Pearl was, in fact, Ellie's home. While in London Ellie had missed her grand desperately, but they stayed in contact via video calls several times a week and via daily text message. Ellie went home when she could, which wasn't often because she was so busy in London, and Pearl rarely left Cornwall because she had her café to run. Despite this, Ellie knew her gran loved her and she knew her gran felt loved. True family loved you no matter what.

But now, at last, she was packed and ready to leave, waiting for her Uber to arrive and transport her to the train station. She let herself out of Barnaby's home for what she knew was the last time, and she dragged her two large suitcases along the winding path. Spring was in the air, and it gave her a sense of hope because it heralded in a new beginning for her. This was a fresh start in her life, a leaving behind of the dreams she used to have as she moved forwards to embrace a new adventure.

Ellie Cordwell was going home, and spring was on the way.

6
PEARL

After Pearl had walked to the garden café, she went around the back of the small building and let herself into the utility area where she kept things like the chicken feed, the birdseed, and garden tools. She located the chicken feed and filled a bucket with cold water, then she went back outside and crossed the garden to the chicken run.

She unlocked the gate to the large walk-in chicken run, then closed it behind her and opened the door to the coop. The rooster emerged first, large with glossy black feathers that seemed almost blue in some lights. His tail feathers were mainly black, but there were a few red and blue ones in there, too. His comb was red and fleshy, and his wattles hung below his beak like two deflated scarlet balloons.

'Morning, gorgeous boy. How're you?' she asked. 'Looking pretty good, Chris Hensworth!'

The rooster strutted around on his sturdy legs, looking like he'd been in the gym working out, and he exuded confidence and arrogance. He kept a watchful eye on his ladies, and

Pearl knew he'd defend them should any predators come near.

'Now where are your pretty hens?' she asked, and as if on cue, he crowed and the chickens began trooping out of the coop too. When they spotted Pearl, they started clucking and gathering around her legs, keen to have their breakfast.

All rescue chickens, they were a variety of White Stars, Marans and Lohman Browns.

'Hello there Princess Lay-a, Buffalo Wings, Chick Pea, Pecky Pudding, Eggs Benedict, Sunny Side Up, Poultry Geist, and Quackelina Jolie.' The chickens trotted around her excitedly as if they knew their names, which Pearl sometimes believed they did, or perhaps it was just that they liked it when she talked to them.

After she'd filled the feeders and changed their water, she tidied up a bit, then let herself out of the run and locked it behind her. Before walking away, she double-checked the lock, aware from experience that not doing so could lead to the chickens escaping into the café gardens.

This was fine as long as the external gates to the gardens were closed, but it became a problem if the chickens got onto the road. The last thing she wanted was for any of them to get hurt or lost.

She returned to the café with the chicken feed that she stored back in the cupboard and she got out the wild birdseed. The bird feeders were a combination of some that hung from trees, some raised bird tables and some ground feeders for the pigeons. The feeders attracted a variety of birds throughout the year, depending on the seasons. Pearl liked to feed them all. It was, she thought, her way of helping nature out, which made her feel like she was doing something useful.

Once Pearl had fed the chickens and birds, she refilled the birdbaths located around the gardens with fresh water, returned everything to the utility room at the rear of the café, then went inside. After she had washed her hands and swapped her wellies for her sheepskin boots again, she went to the kitchen and put the kettle on. She made a coffee and while the ovens heated up; she perched on a stool at the kitchen island and wrote some plans for the week. At the café, she cherished this time of day for thinking and planning.

The day passed quickly, and soon it was late afternoon. This time of day saw a different group of customers because it was when parents frequented the café with their children after school. Thora Mason, one of Pearl's employees was in the kitchen clearing up, and Pearl was out front serving.

The door opened, and Jasper Holmes entered. He was a lovely local man and had two adorable children, seven-year-old Mabel and five-year-old Alfie. Jasper was a polite and quiet man, and Pearl often found herself worrying about him. He had been tragically widowed three years ago just after Christmas, when his wife, Kimberley Wu-Holmes, had been killed in a road traffic accident on her way to work. She'd been a consultant anaesthetist at a local hospital and a very clever and talented person. Kimberley had often visited the café with the children on her days off, and Pearl had liked her a lot. She'd been one of those people who had a glow about them, something that radiated goodness and kindness, and Pearl had been certain that Kimberley would have been excellent at her job. A petite woman with a shiny black bob and dark eyes, Kimberley could seem very serious at times, but once you got to know her, she was warm and funny. Jasper and Kimberley had been a beautiful couple. Their love for one another had been clear, as had their adoration of their two children. Pearl knew Kimberley worked long hours and was very dedicated to her job, but Kimberley was also dedicated to her family, and that made her tragic end all the sadder. Kimberley was a loss to her family, to the village, and to the patients she treated.

As Jasper settled his children at the table near the window where they debated over who would sit on the comfy dark green leather sofa, Pearl watched them from behind the counter. Jasper was a handsome man with his fair hair cropped close to his head in a way that made Pearl think of a U.S. Marine. He had a blonde beard dusted with some whites that caught the light on a sunny day, piercing blue eyes the colour of bright spring skies, shoulders broad enough to carry the weight of a lorry and still accelerate like a sports car, and he was well over six feet tall. In fact, Pearl thought he must be around six-four and he towered over most people. She often thought he reminded her of a big golden bear, the type of bear she might read about in one of the paranormal romance novels she so enjoyed. He looked like he could transform at any moment into a bear shifter, and it was no wonder that many of the single women in the village, and some men, swooned every time he walked into a room. But Jasper wasn't just attractive, he was also a good person. He would do anything for anyone if they asked, but he never, ever, imposed upon others. Over the last three years, this had worried Pearl, because she had been concerned that he might be struggling with his grief, that he might be struggling as a single parent, and that he might be lonely. But whenever she had tried to speak to Jasper about these things, he had shaken his head and closed his eyes momentarily before meeting her gaze and replying that he was just fine. Pearl knew this probably wasn't true, but she also knew that you could only help someone if they wanted to be helped. So she was as kind to him as she could be whenever she saw him, and she was equally kind to the children because the poor mites had lost their mum when they were little more than babies.

Pearl finished serving the customer in front of her, then waited for Jasper to come to the counter. When he did, he smiled at her in the way that made his face briefly light up and her heart squeezed because she wished he could smile this way every day.

'Hello Jasper. How are you today?'

'Not bad thanks, Pearl.' He glanced over at where his children were sitting next to each other on the sofa now, looking at a book they'd got off the shelf behind them. 'Thank goodness those two decided to sit together. There's nothing worse than dealing with an argument over who's going to sit where when there's plenty of room for both of them.' He laughed as he met her eyes. 'Of course, they both say that they want to sit next to me, but I suspect that's just so I'll make the decision about who sits on the sofa.'

'And you could never decide between them, obviously,' Pearl said.

'Never in a month of Sundays.' He shook his head and gazed over at the children, his expression softening in the way it did whenever he looked at them or spoke about them. 'They are my absolute world.' His hand moved to his chest unconsciously as if to rest above his heart, and Pearl felt a lump rising in her throat. It seemed so unfair that this beautiful young man had lost his wife and that their children had lost their mother, but as Pearl knew well, there was no rhyme or reason to the cards life dealt. No rhyme or reason at all.

She served Jasper and he made his way back to his children with the tray of drinks, then returned for the cakes he had ordered for the three of them. There was a buttered tea cake for Jasper, a chocolate eclair for Mabel, and a strawberry doughnut for Alfie. Jasper turned to walk back to the table just as the door to the café opened and, along with the gust of fresh air, came a surprise.

'My goodness!' Pearl exclaimed as she set her eyes on the person who had just walked into the café. 'I had no idea you would be visiting today.'

The woman's eyes flickered to Jasper where he had frozen on his way to the table. It was like time stood still and the air in the café crackled with electricity. Perhaps Pearl had been reading too many paranormal romance novels, but she was convinced that something palpable passed between Jasper and the new arrival.

And then, as with all moments, that one passed on and normality resumed. Jasper went to his table and the woman approached the counter, dragging two large suitcases in her wake. The suitcases looked heavy but suggested Ellie might be home for a while, which excited her.

'Hello Gran,' Ellie said with a big smile but it didn't quite reach her eyes.

'Hello yourself.' Pearl came around the counter and placed her hands on her granddaughter's shoulders. 'It's so good to see you, my darling.' She opened her arms and Ellie let go of the suitcase handles and hugged her gran hard.

'Oh Gran,' Ellie mumbled against Pearl's shoulder. 'I have missed you.'

'I've missed you too.' Pearl hugged Ellie tight, breathing in her amber and vanilla perfume and the coconut conditioner she'd used on her hair. 'But ... I didn't know you were coming home.'

'Neither did I until recently and then I wasn't sure when I'd be back so I thought I'd surprise you. And here I am.' Ellie smiled again, but her green eyes were cloudy.

'For long?' Pearl asked.

Ellie's gaze dropped to the floor and she worried her bottom lip. 'I'm not sure. For a while ... whatever a while is.'

'OK, my darling, well take a seat and you can tell me all about it.'

'Thanks, Gran, but I'm exhausted. Would it be OK if I go back to the cottage and take a nap?'

As much as she wanted to spend time with her granddaughter and to find out what had happened, Pearl could see the dark shadows under Ellie's eyes and feel the tension in her shoulders. Her granddaughter needed rest above all things.

'Of course, Ellie. You head back and I'll catch up with you later. But sit down while I pack you something to eat and make you a warm drink to take with you. Also, you need some help with those cases, so I'll call you a taxi. I'm guessing that's how you got here from the station?'

'Yes.' Ellie sank onto a chair and sighed. 'Thanks, Gran.'

'It's my pleasure.' Pearl went back behind the counter where she rang a local taxi firm, then set about making Ellie a sandwich and a takeaway tea.

If Ellie was staying for a while, then there would be plenty of time to talk about things and plenty of time for her to look after her granddaughter. She had a feeling that Ellie needed some proper Cornish TLC. The type of TLC that a loving grandmother was best able to provide.

7
JASPER

*J*asper sat with his children in the café and listened to their conversation about the book they'd selected from the shelf. It was an encyclopaedia of strange and unusual creatures, and one they had looked at on previous visits, but that never failed to amuse them. It featured a variety of different creatures that would probably not have come to the children's attention without the book they were currently reading. Or, of course, without one of those persistent videos that flashed up on Facebook reels or Instagram. Not that Jasper allowed his two young children to spend much time on social media, but now and then they would ask to borrow his phone or they would switch the television to the YouTube channel. By searching for weird creatures, the algorithms would show them a variety of videos that they found fascinating. It wasn't just strange and unusual creatures that fascinated his children, though, they could spend hours laughing about funny dog antics. The bulldog videos, especially those with dogs dressed as superheroes or in seasonal outfits, particularly delighted them. In one bulldog video they'd watched repeatedly, the bulldog was capable of drying his own mouth on a towel after having a drink. They also liked watching videos about people encountering wild animals when they were walking or hiking along mountain paths. Jasper thought these types of videos should have been scary to his children, but it seemed not, and it did make him wonder about what they saw when they weren't with him. He knew some of their friends had mobile phones and he knew that they took them into school or out with them when they played at the weekends. It was impossible to protect Mabel and Alfie all the time from everything, but he did what he could and to the best of his ability. He was aware that as the children got older and went off to high school, open dialogue with him about the things they watched and the things they spoke about with their friends would be important. At least that way, he could explain anything confusing or unclear to them.

But right now, as they discussed exactly how a jellyfish could eat, he found his gaze drawn to the woman who had entered the café as he had been carrying their cakes to the table. Jasper wasn't in the habit of noticing anyone, let alone women, but there was something about this woman that had made him stop in his tracks. He didn't know her, or at least he didn't think he did, and yet there was something about her that was familiar. He was trying to work out where he might have seen her before, but it seemed to be just outside of his grasp. While he was thinking about this, he saw Pearl hug the younger woman in a way that suggested affection and familiarity, and then it hit him. He had seen the woman before, but not in the flesh. He'd seen her in the photographs on the pin board in the café. She was in quite a lot of photographs with Pearl, therefore she might well be a relative, or at least a very close friend.

He glanced at his children for a moment to check they weren't getting sticky fingers all over the book, and then he looked across the café at Pearl and the woman again. Pearl said something to her before going behind the counter and making a phone call. Meanwhile, the woman sank onto a chair in a way that suggested extreme weariness. Knowing exactly how that kind of exhaustion felt, Jasper wondered what had happened to this woman to make her so tired. Had she lost someone too? Had she been to hell and back? He knew how caring Pearl could be; he knew because Pearl had tried on many occasions to take care of him. Being Jasper, he had pulled back and been unable to talk to Pearl about his feelings, and unable to accept more than the refreshments Pearl could offer him at the café, but her kindness had not gone unnoticed. Her kindness had, on occasion, been as good as a hug from a dear friend, because sometimes, just knowing that people cared was an enormous comfort. Pearl also had a way about her that meant she wasn't afraid of talking about difficult things like loss. Many people who had known him and Kimberley tended to avoid saying her name as if it would remind him she was gone. But he was well aware, every single minute of every single day, that his wife was no longer around. Therefore, to have someone actually say her name and acknowledge her existence was a relief. He would always be grateful to Pearl for saying his wife's name, for admitting that she was a great loss, and for caring enough to try to help him and the children.

He turned back to the table and ate his tea cake, enjoying the salty butter contrasting with the fruit baked into the sweet bread, then drank his coffee. He'd been coming to the café for years and in that time he had never eaten or drunk anything there that was anything less than delicious. Pearl ran the perfect café, and it was, within its beautiful gardens and so close to the sea, the perfect place to go whatever the weather was like.

From the corner of his eye, he saw Pearl hand the young woman a paper bag containing what he assumed was a sandwich, and a recyclable cup, then they made their way to the door, each pulling one of the large suitcases behind them. They hugged again, then the woman opened the door, and they left the café and trundled the suitcases along the winding path out to the road.

A flicker of disappointment pierced his protective veneer as he wondered where the young woman was going. Was she leaving the village now and heading off on a holiday somewhere? Was she going home — wherever that was? He really wasn't in the habit of caring what people did these days, but he found himself wanting to know more about her. He told himself it was because of what he had seen in her eyes and on her face, as well as the weary way she had sunk onto the chair. What kind of monster would he be if he didn't think about what had happened to someone who was clearly in some kind of pain?

It couldn't possibly be anything else rousing his curiosity.

Jasper was married.

Jasper loved his wife.

Jasper was a devoted father with a full-time job.

Jasper was nursing a broken heart, and it was a heart he could not imagine ever being healed. Therefore, his interest in the woman was nothing more than curiosity and compassion. Jasper had no room in his life or his heart for anything else at all, and he was 100% convinced that he never would.

8

ELLIE

The taxi dropped Ellie off at her gran's cottage. She went inside and parked the suitcases in the hallway at the bottom of the wooden staircase. During the long train journey back to Cornwall, that had involved several changes and some delays, she'd felt all right. When she got to the café, however, something had changed, and she'd suddenly felt overwhelmed by exhaustion. A bit like someone had removed her batteries so she was running on empty. It was almost as if seeing her gran had been such an enormous relief that the adrenaline propelling her forwards for the past few weeks had left her body immediately, which meant she had nothing left to keep her going.

She went through a doorway on her right and looked around the pretty lounge. The room was the same as she remembered, with two fat blue sofas covered in crochet patchwork blankets and a small coffee table covered by circular wooden coasters that a friend of her gran's had brought back from Canada. On the low table were five books that her gran was probably reading — she never read one book at a time, always at least three, several notebooks, and a chipped mug filled with a variety of pens. The mug was missing the handle and there was a chip on the rim, but it made Ellie smile because she knew why her gran had kept it. Flowers and the words "If grandmothers were flowers, you'd be the one I'd pick" decorated the side of the mug. Ellie had bought the mug for her gran when she was on a school trip to Helston. She had picked it up in a gift shop and wrapped it up carefully in a tea towel that she'd also bought, then tucked it into her rucksack. She had spent all day — as they wandered around the town, visited local places of interest, and then travelled back on the bus — taking care of the mug like it was a fragile egg. It had been imperative for her to ensure that the mug was not broken and she had succeeded in getting it home safely. When she had given the mug to her gran, the response had made her so proud and happy. Seeing her gran's face light up made her hard work that day in looking after the mug totally worth it. Her gran had kept the mug all these years and used it daily, until one morning, while washing it in the sink, it had bumped against a plate and the handle had come off. This had saddened them both at the time, but then her gran had said she would keep the mug and use it for a different purpose, and so she had done. It had become a pen pot and therefore received a new lease of life. Her gran had a habit of doing the same with other things and if she could up-cycle something instead of buying new, she would do so in a heartbeat.

Ellie wandered around the room, admiring the full bookshelves, the family photographs, the candlesticks on the mantelpiece above the open fireplace, and even the basket of logs on the hearth. The room smelt of rosemary and lavender, of wood smoke and lemon furniture polish, all scents that she associated with her gran's home. All scents she associated with home, because her home had always been with Pearl. Being back here made her realise how much she had missed it and how important this cottage was to her and to who she was. Apart from a few flying visits, she hadn't been back here for any significant amount of time in about three years, possibly four. Now she was here, she couldn't understand why.

Why had she let life become so busy that she hadn't come home?

Why had she allowed Barnaby to convince her that going home to Cornwell for holidays wasn't a good idea?

Why had she not come home to see her gran and to show that she cared enough to make the effort?

She suspected that she knew why, and it did not sit comfortably with her. She had not come back because she had worried it would enable her to think clearly and to see clearly, and by doing so, her life and how unsatisfactory it had become would be evident. If this clarity had confronted her, then it would have been harder for her to go back to London, to continue attending auditions, and to keep hoping Ramona would find it in her heart to like Ellie. It would have become impossible to continue living with Barnaby and pretending, because that was what it had become, to love him still. But now she was home, and she could finally accept that she had been living a lie for quite some time. What she needed to do was to accept that things had not been right and to try to move on with her life by deciding what came next.

But first, she would eat the delicious-looking sandwich that her gran had given her, drink the tea, and take a nap, because she was bone weary.

Despite everything that had happened recently and how difficult she had found it, she really was glad to be home.

9
PEARL

When Pearl got home that evening, the lamps in the lounge and the hallway created a golden glow in the windows that she hadn't come home to for quite some time. The cottage was warm with the presence of another human being and she could hear music playing somewhere inside. She wandered through the hallway, hung her coat on the hook and went through to the lounge. There was no sign of Ellie, but the fire was lit and the room felt like somebody else had been in there recently. Pearl enjoyed living alone and was not afraid of it, but knowing one of her loved ones was in the cottage was lovely.

She left the lounge and went through to the kitchen, enjoying the smells of coffee and toast that greeted her. Ellie wasn't in there either and the back door was closed, so her granddaughter must be upstairs. Not wanting to startle Ellie, she called out a few times to let her know she was there, but there was no response, so she got out her phone and sent Ellie a text. Ellie replied immediately to say she was taking a bath.

Pearl made herself a cup of tea then sat in the lounge. At seventy-five, she was fit and healthy, but after a full day's work she sometimes felt an ache deep in her bones and a tiredness she hadn't experienced when she was younger. She tried to stay fit by doing yoga, some free weights and walking every day, but regardless of that, she was sometimes conscious of the fact that she wasn't getting any younger. She sank onto the sofa and let herself relax; her mug of tea cradled between both hands.

She tilted her head as she tried to work out what Ellie was listening to. And then it became clear. She could hear the beautiful voice of Karen Carpenter as she sang mournfully about rainy days and Mondays. Pearl had always liked the Carpenters and played them regularly while Ellie was growing up, and it seemed that her granddaughter still liked to listen to the band. That was the thing with music — it didn't matter how old you were, what decade you were born in, or what you had been through in your life, it could be timeless. Music brought people together, it comforted them when they were low, and it could lift them higher when they were feeling good. Pearl had always enjoyed music and over the years she'd listened through a variety of mediums. Back in the 1960s and '70s she'd had her record player and listened to her favourites on vinyl. In the '80s she had used vinyl and also cassette tapes then this progressed to audio CDs in the '90s when she was able to afford a CD player. As technology had advanced, she had moved to using apps on her phone that she listened to through portable speakers. When she reflected on it, the rapid changes were astonishing, and she was certain her husband would be astounded by modern technology such as smartphones, iPads, contactless payments, online shopping, and the convenience of purchasing items nowadays. He would have been very impressed, she knew, and she wished with all her heart that she could share these things with him. But then she could also imagine hearing his voice if he caught her browsing Etsy or another online retailer and spending money. Her husband had not liked to spend money, but she was the complete opposite. Pearl loved to shop, she loved to find bargains and beautiful things that she could bring into her home. She liked to avoid new things though, and preferred vintage, recycled and up-cycled, because it was better for the planet. The furniture in the café was up-cycled, as were the paintings that adorned the walls, the shelves that held the books, and even the floorboards were all reclaimed or up-cycled. It was, Pearl thought, one of the things that made the café such a pleasant place to be, such a cosy and homely environment. She also liked to buy second-hand books when she visited charity shops, although not wanting to take away sales from authors, she then bought a copy of the books for her e-reader so she was supporting the authors who needed to make a living too. Pearl believed that up-cycled, recycled and vintage goods were more interesting than brand new items because they had a history. Before they had come into her possession, they had been somewhere else, with someone else, serving a different purpose perhaps than they were now. And she liked to think that after her time, someone else would then take these things on and give them a whole new life. There was comfort in this just as in the passing of the seasons, because it meant that life went on, people went on, items went on, and there was continuity. Human beings were but a speck on the earth, a minuscule part of the universe, and while they were important to their loved ones, they were just a part of something far bigger. She was a part of something far more significant than one brief human life. Pearl would live on, through the energy she left behind and through her daughter and her granddaughter. Granted, she saw little of her daughter these days, so she wasn't sure how much of a legacy she would leave there, but she was close to Ellie and knew that Ellie would remember her.

Hearing a noise, she looked towards the doorway and smiled when her granddaughter appeared, as if her thoughts about Ellie had conjured her.

'Ellie darling,' she said. 'How are you now?'

'Much better for some sleep and a bubble bath,' Ellie replied as she towelled off her hair. 'I really needed to catch up on some rest. I haven't been sleeping great lately, and it was so nice to come home and to snuggle up in my old bed.'

'You found the sheets easily enough, then?' The bed hadn't been made-up in the spare room, or rather Ellie's room, because Ellie hadn't been home in some time. Pearl hadn't seen the point in leaving the sheets on the bed just to get dusty so she'd left the bed stripped and the sheets tidied away.

'Yes, of course. Everything was in the airing cupboard... washed, ironed, smelling of sunny days and of lavender. I see you've still got the dried lavender bunches in there. Also, when I got the sheets out of the airing cupboard to make up the bed, they were warm, so I couldn't wait to slip between them. I wasn't particularly dirty because I showered this morning but I was feeling a bit stale from the journey. It's funny how travelling and tiredness can make you feel that way.'

Pearl smiled at her granddaughter, enjoying listening to her while gazing at her in person. It was one thing being able to video call, but it was a whole other treat to see her granddaughter in the flesh and to have her staying under her roof once more.

'Did you eat?' she asked.

Ellie nodded. 'I had the sandwich you made for me, which was delicious by the way, and I had the tea but I was still a bit peckish, so I had a look in the cupboards and found some chocolate biscuits.' Ellie grinned mischievously. 'Then some coffee and toast. I hope that was OK.'

'Of course, it's OK, darling! What's mine is yours. It's always been that way. Surely you know that?'

'I do. Thank you, Gran... It's so good to be home.'

'It's good to have you home. I have missed you, but I don't like to put pressure on you by telling you that when you're in London. I know you have a whole life there to live and the last thing I want is for you to be worrying about me missing you.' Pearl's vision blurred slightly, and she blinked hard. 'It's important that you feel happy and confident enough to head off into the world and to live your life without worrying about me or this place or anything else at all.' She looked at her granddaughter and concern washed over her because Ellie had gone quite pale. 'What is it? What's wrong?'

Ellie wrapped the towel around her neck, sucked in a shaky breath, and rubbed her cheeks. 'My so-called successful life in London is actually not that at all. In fact, it's very far from successful.'

'Whatever has happened, darling?' Pearl asked softly.

'Gran, I'll tell you, but I'm so worried you'll be disappointed in me. I mean, I know I've told you over the years that things are going well and-and sometimes they have been going well... but-but more recently, everything seems to have gone wrong.' Ellie's bottom lip wobbled, making her look like a little girl and she rubbed her cheeks again.

'Look darling, why don't I make us a drink,' Pearl said, placing her mug on the coffee table, 'and then you can tell me all about it?'

'That would be great, Gran.' Ellie looked down at herself as if realising she was wearing her dressing gown and a towel. 'I'll just go and put my pyjamas on.'

'You do that and I'm going to make us a gin and tonic. I think we both need it.' Pearl stood up, picked up her mug and crossed the room, pausing to watch as Ellie climbed the stairs. 'Whatever it is, Ellie, we can fix it. I promise you that. Nothing is too difficult to fix.'

Ellie sniffed and nodded. 'Thanks, Gran. I don't know what I'd do without you.'

As Pearl went to the kitchen, she said softly to herself, 'I don't know what I'd do without you, either, my darling girl.'

10

JASPER

*E*venings were busy as a single parent. There was no getting away from it. From the moment Jasper collected the children from school, it was all go, until he got them safely tucked into bed. And then there were other jobs to do — washing, ironing, getting uniforms ready for the next day, making packed lunches, cleaning (although vacuuming was out then as it was too noisy, so he tried to do that during the day). With a partner, these jobs were split, and things worked more smoothly, or they had done when Kimberley had been alive. Even though they'd both had jobs and the children, they'd kept the house running like a well-oiled machine. Plus, of course, there were other things like having someone to sit with during the evenings. They'd eat together at the table if they hadn't eaten earlier with the children and talk about their days, the people they'd encountered (mainly online in Jasper's case), and share stories to make each other laugh. Sometimes, they'd take their food and perhaps a bottle of wine through to the lounge and snuggle on the sofa, limbs entwined, and enjoy being close. Even when they'd sat together in silence, it had been comforting just knowing she was there. To feel her warmth and to hold her had been incredible. Jasper missed that intimacy because life could be hard and having someone, your person, in your corner, was unbeatable. But to have that and lose it was, he sometimes thought, possibly worse than never having it at all, because he knew exactly what he was missing. And he missed it, missed her, so much.

And so here he was again, packing lunch boxes for the next day and rattling around the large open-plan kitchen alone while his children slept upstairs. He put the lunchboxes into the fridge, then washed his hands and stood by the bifold doors that opened out onto the garden. From here, he could see the moon climbing the sky and the silvery light it cast over the sea. The areas of the water not bathed in the moonlight were dark and seemed fathomless, while the moon seemed to light up a pathway that led along the centre of the water like an ethereal ribbon. It made Jasper think about how life could be when you had a partner. Your relationship could be a safe path that led you through life, a place where light glowed, while surrounding your love there were dark places you never wanted to fall into. But without Kimberley, Jasper was teetering on the edge of the silver, held there only by the remnants of their love, almost tipping into the bleakness of loneliness and grief. What would it take for him to fall into the darkness completely?

'Dammit!' He shook himself and rubbed his hands over his beard. All this thinking about what he'd lost was counterproductive. It was hard to move on, even after three years, but he was trying to be strong for the children. He was trying so hard. He had to be strong for them.

His phone pinged with an alert that someone was at the door, so he picked it up and peered at the screen. Standing on his doorstep were Daniel Forsythe and Naveen Malik. The two men were waving at the doorbell camera and Naveen held up a box of beer.

Jasper took a breath before going to answer the door. Daniel and Naveen were local men who'd tried to get him to go out for a beer on many occasions over the years, but he always had an excuse not to go. However, they never stopped trying, as if hoping that one day they'd convince him. They'd also tried to encourage him to go for walks and hikes, to meet up on the beach with their children (which he had done several times) and to go out for dinner with their partners and some friends. Jasper had been worried that 'some friends' meant single women looking for love, and so he'd stood his ground and refused to go, but the men hadn't seemed to take offence at his refusal. They really did seem like genuinely nice people, and he liked them, but he'd kept himself as distant as he could because letting people in terrified him.

He opened the front door, holding Wiggy's collar with one hand, and pressed a finger to his lips then pointed above his head so they'd know the children were in bed.

'Both sleeping?' Naveen asked.

'Yes, thankfully.' Jasper laughed. 'You guys want to come inside?'

They followed him through to the kitchen and Naveen set the beers down on the island. 'These are cold,' he said. 'I got them straight out of the fridge at the shop. Want one?'

'Don't mind if I do,' Daniel said, but he paused mid reach. 'Jasper, is this OK? We don't want to impose, but we thought you might like some company.'

'Yes!' Jasper nodded. 'Yes, it's fine. I was just making packed lunches and about to start the ironing, but hey … having company is much better.' He smiled, but he wasn't sure he sounded convincing enough. The last thing he wanted was to offend Naveen and Daniel because they were making an effort, and anyway, it would be nice to have some company. He was getting far too stuck in his ways and things had to change somewhere or he'd become a total recluse. The children would grow up and he'd be left home alone, a widower with no friends and no one to turn to except for his children, and who wanted to end up like that? It wouldn't be fair on them or, for that matter, on him. And it also wouldn't be what Kimberley would have wanted for him. Not. At. All. That wasn't who Kimberley had been, and it wasn't who Jasper had been when he was with her. Perhaps this was a sign that it was time for him to start, or at least to try to start, making some changes to how he was living his life.

'Excellent.' Naveen held out a beer and Jasper looked at it for a moment, then shook his head.

'It's fine. I'll have a coffee.'

'You sure?' Naveen asked, tilting his head slightly.

'Let the man have coffee, if that's what he wants. I'll have a coffee too,' Daniel said. 'If that's OK?'

Jasper smiled then and shook his head. 'Tell you what, I'll take a beer. But just one, as I have to be up early with the children. I find it hard to relax on a school night.'

'I can understand that.' Naveen held out a bottle of beer. 'And that's why these are very low alcohol.'

Wiggy had been politely sniffing the new arrivals but as if

realising they hadn't brought anything for him, he went to his bed and settled down.

Jasper accepted the bottle and read the label. 'That's cool. All the taste and less alcohol, perfect for a weeknight.'

'Exactly!' Naveen said as the three of them clinked beers.

They sat around the kitchen island on the high stools and Jasper told himself to relax. There was nothing to feel anxious about and nothing to worry about. Naveen and Daniel had wanted to come here to spend time with him, and that was all good.

'So, Jasper ... We've tried for a while to get you to come out with us and to arrange something that doesn't involve children and the beach, lol, but you've resisted so far. There is absolutely no pressure on you at all, but we want you to know that we are here for you.' Daniel met Jasper's gaze and he could see the concern in the man's eyes. 'Not in a funny way, you know, that might make you feel uncomfortable, but we like you and want you to know we're here.'

Naveen nodded. 'It's true. I mean, how long have we known you now?' He frowned. 'Three ... no, four years?'

'About that.' Jasper nodded.

'And when you first moved here, you were always busy with your family, just like us, but then you lost...' Naveen winced. 'Sorry. Didn't mean to bring that up—'

'Please don't be sorry.' Jasper took a swig of beer, suddenly wishing it was stronger. 'People are often afraid to talk about Kimberley. It's like they think saying her name will remind me of what I lost. But the thing is ... I never forget. I think about her and how much I miss her every second of every day. I dream about her all the time. She's gone, but she'll always be in my life. I see her in the children, in our home and, well … in everything I do. That's the thing with losing your partner, they're never really gone, you know?'

'Of course.' Naveen nodded solemnly.

'I am sorry,' Daniel said. 'It must be so hard. Julia, is my world. And the kids, of course.'

Daniel and Julia had three children. They'd started dating at high school and been together ever since. Naveen was married to Pete, who taught at the village primary school.

'Yeah, and Pete is mine,' Naveen said, placing his beer on the island. 'The thought of losing him … it takes my breath away. So while I can't pretend to know what you're going through, I can imagine how awful it must be.'

Jasper nodded slowly. 'Yeah … it's pretty awful.' He smiled at them both. 'But I'm grateful for your kindness. It really helps, even if I don't always show it.'

'We're here for you, buddy,' Daniel said. 'Anything we can do, you just have to ask.'

'It's true.' Naveen picked up his bottle again.

'I really appreciate that.' Jasper swigged his beer. 'So please never be afraid to say Kimberley's name and never feel you need to walk on eggshells around me. I won't break.'

'Good to know.' Naveen drained his bottle. 'Now who's for another beer?'

He passed them all a bottle and Jasper finished the first one before opening the next. He'd never had other men sitting around his kitchen island like this, and he found he was enjoying it far more than he'd have expected. They spent the next hour talking about a range of subjects like football scores (not something he had much interest in, but he knew enough to weigh in when Manchester United fan Naveen waxed lyrical about the team's performance), what was happening politically in America (some of it rather unsettling), how the children were getting on at school and spring events coming up in the village. It was good to talk, and Jasper felt himself unwinding. The thing with being alone and not having anyone at home to speak to other than the children was that it could get lonely. It could be hard, and he often ended up too lost in his own thoughts. Adult company was important, and he was very aware of how much he had missed it and how uplifting it could be just to talk to people who understood and who were at the same stage of life as him. Yes, they hadn't lost their partners, but they had been through other losses — grandparents, parents, and friends — and so there was some understanding of the grieving process.

'The thing is, Jasper,' Naveen said, 'People often say time's a healer, but I don't really agree with that. Time doesn't heal so much as provide us with a chance to make space in our lives for grief. It allows us to accept that the grief will always be a part of our lives and to learn to live with it. I miss my dear old Nanna terribly and she passed away when I was fifteen. She lived with us, and she was a huge part of my life. When she passed away in her late seventies, I was devastated. That was seventeen years ago, but I can still hear her voice, smell her lavender perfume, and remember how it felt to hug her. She was a tiny woman, but she had the biggest personality and when she died, she left a huge space in our lives. It takes time to get used to that space and to process the fact that someone is gone. I think we keep expecting to wake up and find it was all a dream and that they'll walk through the door. But, of course, that doesn't happen. It can't happen. Doesn't stop us wishing it would though. It's OK to feel that way and it's perfectly normal too.' He gazed over at the bifold doors and Jasper followed his gaze to where the moon had shifted position, now highlighting another area of the sea. 'Yup … grief changes, but it never leaves us.'

'I'm sorry for your loss,' Jasper said. 'However long ago it was doesn't matter. Loss is loss.'

'Thanks.' Naveen nodded. 'And I am very, very sorry for yours.'

Daniel got up and walked over to the doors. 'Cracking view this, Jasper.' He gestured at the sea. 'You know what? I think that it's OK to lean on other people. We've all loved and lost and will continue to do so as life moves on. It's inevitable that we'll lose loved ones along the way. And one day, who knows when, we'll be gone too. But leaning on others is fine. People need people and we are here to support you, Jasper, and one another.'

'Thanks.' Jasper nodded. 'It really does mean a lot.'

He got up and joined Daniel at the doors and Naveen followed him, then the three of them gazed out at the view. They stood there for a while, silently supporting one another. Sometimes, silent support was as good as that filled with words. And a funny thing happened. Jasper felt the tension in his shoulders crack like someone had taken a hammer to a block of ice, and a few chips fell away. It was a weird feeling, and he rolled his shoulders as if to shake it off. That didn't happen, of course, because three years of grief had tightened his shoulders right up. But just to be aware of a slight easing there was incredible.

'I don't know about you guys, but I'm a bit peckish,' Jasper said. 'You fancy some nachos?'

'I thought you'd never ask,' Naveen said with a chuckle.

'Sounds perfect.' Daniel grinned. 'Point me toward the cheese grater and I'll help.'

Jasper led the way, feeling lucky to have two friends to support him, just as he would support them. Everyone had to start somewhere, and this was, he thought, a step in the right direction.

11
ELLIE

*L*egs tucked underneath her on the sofa, blanket wrapped around her and gin and tonic in hand, Ellie sighed with contentment. This was how life should be.

'Ooh, that hits the spot!' Her gran raised her glass. 'Here's to discovering new gins and new tonics and enjoying them!' She winked at Ellie. 'But most of all, here's to having my beautiful granddaughter home for a while.'

'Cheers, Gran.' Ellie raised her glass, then took a sip. She coughed. 'Gosh, that's strong!'

'Too much tonic drowns the flavour of the gin, darling.' Her gran chuckled. 'And that's not acceptable at all.'

Ellie took another sip. 'It's delicious. What flavour is it?'

'This is the rhubarb and vanilla gin with elderflower tonic.'

Ellie took another sip, then set the heavy glass down on the coffee table. She had a feeling that if she didn't, she'd keep drinking and it was strong, so she wanted to take her time. 'So how have you been, Gran?'

'I'm good, thanks. Just carrying on as I always do.'

Ellie nodded. 'It's good to be home. I forget when I'm away exactly how much I love the village and this cottage, as well as your strong gin and tonics.'

Pearl laughed. 'It is a lovely place to live and yes, I do make the best G&T I've ever tasted. I can't abide the pub ones you get with a teaspoon of gin and a pint of tonic. Who wants their gin overwhelmed?'

'Well, I don't think gin has done you any harm.' Ellie thought her gran looked phenomenal with her glowing skin, toned figure, and bright eyes. She was seventy-five but looked around twenty years younger, if not more. 'I can't believe you're five years off eighty.'

Pearl shook her head. 'Now we'll have none of that talk, young lady. No one in this house is going to be eighty anytime soon!'

'You can't stop time, Gran.'

'True. But I can *deny* time.' Pearl swigged her drink. 'Only joking, Ellie. You know I'm proud of my age and have never lied about it. I don't understand that. Why would you be ashamed of getting older when being able to age is a gift that not all people get? Look at that beautiful young woman who passed away a few years ago.'

'Who?' Ellie frowned, trying to recall if her gran had mentioned this to her at some point.

'Kimberley Wu-Holmes. She was an intelligent person, an anaesthetist, and a wife and mum. She had everything to live for and then some drugged up wastrel killed her in a car pile up and left her husband and children to manage without her.'

'That's terrible.' Ellie gulped. 'The poor woman and her poor family.'

'Life can be cruel.' Pearl sighed. 'We all lose loved ones but as you get older you expect it, just not when you're as young as Kimberley was. I often think of those poor little children being left without a mum.'

'It's very sad.' Ellie shook her head.

'You might have seen them in the café earlier with their dad,' her gran said. 'Tall, handsome man with short hair and a beard?'

Ellie frowned as she thought back. 'Yes. With two young children sitting by the bookshelves.'

'That's right. Lovely man he is, although he won't let anyone get close.'

Ellie had noticed Jasper and how handsome he was, but it had been a fleeting awareness. She'd been emotional at seeing her gran and at being home in the gorgeous village again, so her *handsome man radar* hadn't been functioning at full capacity.

'And you lost Grampa quite young too,' Ellie said, thinking of his ruddy cheeks and thick white hair, a moustache that tickled when he kissed her cheek. He'd been a big man capable of scooping her up onto his shoulders then walking along the beach with her, pointing out landmarks and telling her myths and legends about the area.

'I did. Not as young as Jasper losing his wife, but too young all the same.' Her gran smiled sadly. 'Feels like it happened yesterday but, of course, it didn't. It'll be twenty years this November.'

'Twenty years ago, that he gave his life to save another.' Ellie thought of that terrible night when they'd had one of the worst storms in years. A local teenager been drinking with his friends, and they'd dared him to cliff dive then swim around the coastline. Naturally, he ran into trouble, and the lifeboat went out to rescue him. During the rescue attempt, three crew members, including her grandpa, were thrown from the boat. He'd helped the other two clamber back in, along with the teenager, but then the current had been too strong and he'd been tired. A wave swept him along, then the swell pulled him under, and the sea claimed him. His friends had tried everything to get him back, but it had been too awful a night and too powerful a storm. It had only been the following day, in the calm that came afterwards, that the search party had found her grampa on a beach further along the coast. He'd been a strong and experienced swimmer, but no human being was a match for the sea when it roared. The sea had to be respected or the consequences could be tragic. 'Are you OK?' she inquired gently.

'I'm OK.' Her gran raised her glass. 'To absent friends, especially my boy. He was always my boy, you know, even though he was older than me. To die like that at sixty was so sad, but knowing him as I did and how much he loved the sea, it was probably the way he'd have wanted to go. He was always an adventurous bugger and liked wild swimming, skiing, rock climbing. What they call an adrenaline junkie now, I guess. But it was one of the things I loved about him. He died a hero, a very brave man. He was such a hunk.' She grinned at Ellie. 'I know you won't want to think about your grampa in that way, but he was hunky, and I adored him.'

'I know you did.' Ellie looked over at the photos of her grampa that adorned the shelves, the mantelpiece, and the walls. Her gran had told her that in his youth he reminded her of Marlon Brando, and he'd only improved with age. Ellie could see why her gran found him so attractive, because he had been handsome, large and masculine. It was what she found attractive in men herself. Ellie ending up with Barnaby was quite odd, actually, because he'd been small and not at all rugged. He'd also been obsessed with his appearance and with taking selfies, which was something else she wasn't fussy about.

'But such is life. I'm grateful that I had him around for as long as I did and that he loved me the way he did.' Her gran sat forwards and placed her glass on the coffee table. 'Anyway, my darling, tell me what brought you home.'

'Sure.' Ellie unfolded her legs and shifted her position on the sofa, then sipped her drink, needing another mouthful of gin before she shared her news. 'Things with Barnaby just came to a head.'

'Go on.' Her gran didn't look surprised, which made Ellie wonder if she'd seen this coming.

'Well ... it all came about because I went for an audition and I think Ramona arranged it to set me up to fail.'

'What? Why would she do that?' Her gran's voice rose as she spoke. 'She was your agent and isn't an agent supposed to have your back?'

'I don't think she ever wanted to sign me, in all honesty, although I wanted to believe she did at the time. She did it as a favour for Barnaby's parents and then she just wanted rid of me at the earliest opportunity.'

'But you were with her for a few years?'

'Yes, but she always sent me to auditions I didn't have a chance of getting. I don't think she liked me.'

'Why wouldn't she like you?' Her gran had her hands on her knees now, sitting on the edge of the sofa as if she would spring forwards at any moment and rush to hunt Ramona down. The tension in her posture was palpable, her muscles coiled like a tightly wound spring awaiting release.

'How could anyone not like you?'

'Well…' Ellie shrugged. 'I'm not everyone's cup of tea and I certainly wasn't hers. Or Barnaby's it seems.'

'Oh darling, their loss is my gain.'

'Thanks, Gran, you always say the kindest things.'

'I love you and can't understand how anyone couldn't love you.'

'The last audition she sent me on was awful. The casting director told me to tap dance, and as you know, I've never done tap dancing before. I decided to improvise and was going for gold when one of my shoes came loose and flew off.'

Her gran covered her mouth with a hand. 'No!'

'Yes. It flew through the air and hit the casting director smack bang in the face.'

'No!' Her gran shook her head, mouth wide open now and hands on her cheeks.

'Yup. Gave her a nosebleed and everything.' Ellie had avoided sharing this information with her gran over the phone because she hadn't wanted her to worry and she'd felt it was best delivered in person. Sharing it now though was a huge relief. She'd never liked keeping things from her gran.

'Goodness! What did you do?'

'Stood there like a lemon while they ushered her off to get it seen to then grabbed my things and left. Without my lost shoe, though.'

'Oh, Ellie, that's awful but kind of…' Her gran bit her lip but her shoulders were shaking. 'K-kind of … f-funny!'

As her gran snorted, Ellie felt laughter bubbling in her belly, and it soon burst out of her. The pair of them laughed until tears were running down their cheeks and their stomachs were aching. When she could catch her breath, Ellie said, 'That's the most I've laughed in ages.'

'Me too. I told you gin is great stuff, didn't I?'

'It is, but it's not just the gin, it's you and how you reacted. I've struggled to see the funny side of what happened, but it is amusing. I mean … my shoe hit her in the face, and she was furious. It was awful at the time, and I felt bad for her, but she was a bit cold towards me before it happened.'

'Perhaps it made her realise you were destined for *shoe-business*. Or that you were *shoe-ting f*or the stars! Who knows?'

They started giggling again, and it took even longer for them to calm down this time.

'Sounds like she had it coming.' Her gran shrugged as she dabbed at her eyes with a tissue. 'If the shoe fits and all that! She might be horrible to everyone she auditions. Some people can get so stuck up their own bottoms with their sense of self-importance that they forget all about what it's like to be human. No one should forget about being kind and compassionate.'

'I agree. When I got home and told Barnaby, he wasn't mad but then he explained why. He had his own news that he was going travelling for a year.'

'Did he ask you to go?'

'Nope. He wanted to go and find himself.'

'Ah well … it's a good job he's got Mummy and Daddy's money to be able to do that, eh?'

'It's true.' Ellie inclined her head. 'It's not cheap finding yourself these days.'

'He's going to do some sole-searching!' Her gran winked. That led to more laughter and Ellie felt the tension of the past few months seeping from her like air from a slowly deflating balloon. It seemed that gin, laughter, and a loving gran were the best medicine, the medicine she had needed without even realising it.

'So you're not going back to him?' her gran asked.

'No. We're done. I did stay on to house-sit, which is why I didn't tell you before now. I was embarrassed it had gone so wrong, and I didn't want to tell you over the phone or by message. Besides which, I wanted to see your face when I told you about #shoe-gate.' Ellie had also wanted the time to mull it over before she told her gran because she hadn't been 100% certain how she felt about it. Until now.

'I'm certainly relishing it.' Her gran sipped her drink. 'The #shoegate bit not the part about your boyfriend being an idiot.'

Ellie sighed. 'Anyway … Ramona let me go and so did my boyfriend and his family, so here I am.'

'What are your plans now? Will you try to find a local agent and audition here?'

'The thought chills me, to be honest, so I want to take some time and think about what comes next.'

'That is very wise of you. Don't rush anything. Just enjoy being home. Breathe. Walk. Eat. Relax. Give yourself some space and it will all become clear in time.'

'I hope so.'

'I know so, my darling. I've been through plenty over the years and time and space always help to clarify your next steps.'

'Thanks, Gran.'

'Right then…' Her gran held up her empty glass. 'Shall we have another drinky-poo and something to eat?'

'That sounds amazing.' Ellie put a hand to her stomach as it growled loudly. 'I'm famished now.'

'Me too. Gin always gives me an appetite.' Her gran stood up and went to the doorway. 'You coming?'

'I certainly am.' Ellie placed the fleecy blanket on the sofa, then stood up, picked up her glass and followed her gran. She paused in the doorway and looked back at the cosy lounge with its curtains drawn, log fire burning, candles lit and lamps glowing in the corners. The large photo of her grampa on the mantelpiece shone in the light. It was almost like he was glowing in the photo, like he was breathing and not just an image captured in a long ago time. But then he lived on in her heart and memories and always would do.

'Come on, darling!' her gran called from the kitchen. 'You can pour the drinks while I whip up some supper.'

'Coming!' Ellie called. She blew a kiss toward her grampa and went to join her gran. 'It is *so* good to be home.'

12
ELLIE

'I can't believe I've been back for Cornwall for two weeks,' Ellie said as she waited for her gran to unlock the door to the café.

'It has certainly flown.' Her gran entered the café and turned the lights on. 'I am enjoying having you home, though, darling.'

'I'm enjoying being home.' Ellie placed the bags she'd carried on one table and grabbed hold of her gran and hugged her. 'I love you so much.'

Her gran chuckled. 'And I love you.'

'I'm sorry I didn't come home more often.'

Her gran patted her shoulder. 'Don't be daft, darling. You were living your life, and I didn't expect you to keep coming back to check on me.'

'I feel terrible that I didn't come back to see you. Like I neglected you.'

And Ellie did. She'd been so wrapped up in her life in London, in trying to please Jasper and his parents, in working at the bar and in trying to secure an acting job that she'd put her gran out of her mind. She'd just assumed that she'd be fine. And Pearl had been fine, but now that she'd been home for a while, Ellie could see the signs that her gran was getting older. She was still fit and healthy, in better shape than many people her age, but she was ageing and nothing could turn back the hands of time. If anything had happened to her gran while she'd been away, she'd never have forgiven herself. Her gran had been there for her when her parents had not; she was Ellie's family.

'I wasn't feeling neglected, Ellie.'

'But I did neglect you and you gave me everything.' Tears welled in Ellie's eyes, blurring her vision and threatening to spill over. Then they did and the salty droplets stung as they cascaded down her cheeks, leaving a trail of dampness in their wake.

'Only my heart, sweeting. I gave you my heart.' Her gran leant back and met her gaze, then stroked Ellie's hair back from her face. 'And I would do it again and again.'

'Oh Gran.' Ellie swallowed against the lump in her throat. 'You're just so wonderful, even after everything you've been through.'

Her gran laughed as she let go of Ellie and unzipped her jacket. 'I don't know about that.'

'But my dad left. You lost Grampa, then Mum ran away to Scotland, and you raised me alone.'

'And that is something I never saw as a problem, Ellie. It has been an honour.' Her gran gestured at the kitchen. 'Let's get the chickens sorted, then we can have a cuppa. They'll all be wanting their breakfast.'

Ellie followed her gran through to the kitchen and the utility room, where she filled a bucket with water while her gran got the chicken feed out of a cupboard.

'Do you ever feel angry with Mum?' Ellie asked as they crossed the grass to the chicken run.

'About what?' Her gran put the food container down, unlocked the gate to the enclosure, then closed it behind them.

'For leaving you after you'd lost your husband.'

'Your mum needed to go. She'd been through a lot. Don't forget, she lost your dad to another woman and that broke her heart and then two years later she lost her dad. A switch flipped in her mind, and she couldn't cope with staying here anymore.'

'So she ran away.' Ellie sighed. She didn't feel bitter or even angry towards her mum for leaving her, but sometimes she wished her mum had been there for her gran.

'Sometimes people need to run away. It's the only way they can cope, and that's what happened with your mum. She needed a change of scenery and to start over. Do I wish she'd done things differently? Sometimes.' Her gran opened the chicken coop, and the rooster emerged, then strutted across the run and stretched his wings. Even in the early morning light, his feathers looked as glossy as if they'd been painted with oil. 'Sometimes, I wish she'd thought more about the impact of her decisions upon *you*.'

'But I turned out fine.' Ellie nudged her gran, and they both laughed.

'It's true. But my wish for you when you were small was that you'd have your mum around. Even a bit closer, perhaps. Scotland is quite a trek from here.'

'It's one hell of a trek.' Ellie shuddered at the thought of the journey to Perth in Scotland that felt like weeks whenever she'd travelled to see her mum. 'No wonder she never came back to see us very often.'

Her gran was filling the feeders, so Ellie got the bucket and changed the water. The chickens gathered around them as if to welcome them. Meanwhile, Chris Hensworth emitted a few loud crows and looked very pleased with himself.

'And what of my dad?' Ellie asked when they'd made a fuss of the birds and were on their way back to the café. 'Do you blame him?'

Her gran stopped walking and turned to Ellie. Behind the café, the sky glowed pink and apricot with the sunrise, and the glow touched her gran's face making her skin look peachy and youthful. For a moment, Ellie could see how her gran would have looked when she was younger, and it tugged at her heart. Once upon a time, her gran had been young with her whole life stretching out ahead of her. She'd fallen in love, had a child and a future with her family to look forward to. But time had passed, and her life had changed beyond recognition, yet here she was, still smiling, still kind and resilient, positive and loving. There was nothing Pearl Draper wouldn't do for anyone because she had the kindest, biggest heart.

'Your dad was a funny one.' Her gran chewed at her bottom lip thoughtfully. 'I liked him. We met when he came here one year on holiday with some friends and he and your mum fell madly in love. They were just sixteen, and it was all very intense. For months, they corresponded, then the following summer he came back and never returned home. They couldn't bear to be apart and I thought they'd be together forever and so did your grampa. Eventually, they got their own place and then your mum got pregnant with you and I guess life just got in the way. They didn't have much money, and we tried to help out but your dad … well, he liked a drink and the horses and so their financial situation got worse and then one day … He upped and left.'

'With another woman.' It wasn't a question because Ellie knew the truth about her dad's infidelity. For years she'd felt betrayed by him because he hadn't just left her mum, he'd left her too. He'd never got in touch, not even on her birthday. It was, she thought, quite clear to her that he had never loved her. But she'd had her gran and her grampa and so she'd never felt like she lacked love. She'd been lucky, she thought, and perhaps that attitude was also something she'd inherited from her gran because her gran was a glass half full kind of person.

'There was another woman … not from here, but she worked at the betting shop he frequented. He took a liking to her and then decided that she would make him happier than your mum did and off he went. Such a shame that he didn't stay in touch. Your mum could have tried to track him down and asked for child support, but she was too proud and wanted nothing to do with him afterwards. We felt so bad for her. But we couldn't push her to pursue him and so we did what we could to support her and you, which was why you moved back in with us. That was a pleasure though, because having you around was, and always has been, an absolute delight.'

'And then Mum fell in love again.'

'Hmmm.' Her gran raised her brows slowly. 'OK, it wasn't an overnight romance, but I still think she was vulnerable. She went on a few dates after joining that dating app and then, when she met Bryce, it was all she talked about for months.'

'Bryce.' Ellie smiled. He was a giant of a man with a bushy grey beard and hair like wire wool. He owned a farm in Perth and always smelt like manure. Her mum adored him and his eyes followed her around whatever room they were in, as besotted as a teenager. And so, even though Ellie had occasionally wished her mum could be around more, she'd also known that her mum had found her *happy ever after* and there was no way anyone could begrudge her that.

'Good old Bryce.' Her gran laughed. 'Come on, let's get that kettle on.'

They went back inside the café and washed their hands, then her gran filled the kettle and made tea while Ellie hung up their coats.

It wasn't like they hadn't spoken about these things before, but sometimes conversations needed to be had more than once to work things through. Perspectives could change with age and experience and sometimes human beings simply needed to get the words out in order to set them free.

'I am happy that Mum's happy,' Ellie said, perched on a stool at the stainless steel island at the centre of the café kitchen.

'Me too. She took your grampa's death very badly. With it coming after your dad had left too, she was even more vulnerable. We're all just trying to get through, Ellie, and have to do what we have to do.'

'I needed to leave London.' Ellie accepted a mug of tea from her gran.

'And you did it at the right time for you.'

Ellie blew on her tea. 'You don't think I should have come home before?'

Her gran shook her head. 'You'd always have wondered if you hadn't given it enough time and that could have led to regrets. Nothing worse than regretting not giving something enough of a chance. That applies to acting and to Barnaby. I think you could return to acting though if your heart still yearns to go in that direction.'

Ellie sipped her tea. 'I'm just not sure. But I don't think it does now. I gave it a shot, and it didn't work out.'

'Yes but that agent of yours wasn't helping. If you got a different agent, it might work out.'

'It could and I'll see how it goes. But right now, I'm enjoying being away from all that pressure. I like working here.' She smiled, thinking about how the last two weeks had been. Working at the café with her gran, was very rewarding. She'd helped out there before, but that was back when she had dreams of being a famous actor and making it big. The idea of working at a Cornish café for life had seemed beneath what she was aiming for and no way near exciting enough. But now that she'd experienced life away from the village and how harsh the world could be, she felt differently. During the past two weeks, she'd enjoyed the lack of pressure on her days, the lack of focus on her appearance and performances, the time to catch up with people from the village and to meet new ones. Despite not wanting to admit it to herself (lest her grandmother guess her thoughts), she enjoyed seeing Jasper Holmes and his children. Had actually looked forward to seeing him come into the café — sometimes with his children and sometimes alone — and anticipated speaking to him again. Their exchanges had been brief, limited to what he wanted to order and to the weather, but still ... he was very handsome with a lovely deep voice. She liked how respectful he was towards others, especially her gran. Barnaby hadn't even wanted to speak to her gran over video calls, but Jasper made eye contact with Pearl and really listened to her, asked about her and offered to help with anything she needed. One day when he'd been there, a delivery had arrived and Ellie and Pearl had tried to get it inside, but it had been too heavy. Jasper had been working on his laptop at the table near the window (the one he always chose if it was free) and when he'd seen them struggling, he'd gone out to help. He lifted the boxes as easily as if they were polystyrene. The delivery driver was new and in a hurry, so he hadn't brought the delivery inside. Ellie had tried not to notice the way the muscles in Jasper's arms had rippled as he'd brought the boxes through the café and into the kitchen, but it was hard not to see how strong he was. She'd caught her gran watching her watching Jasper and had blushed crimson. As a result, she tried not to look at him again, but that proved difficult when he came to the counter to order something. Not looking at him and making eye contact then would seem very rude indeed.

'Well, one day this place will be yours.' Her gran gazed at her over her mug and Ellie shook her head.

'Gran! Don't say things like that.'

'It's true. I've told your mum, and she's fine about it. After all, she had acres and acres in Scotland and doesn't want this place, anyway. Besides, I told her it should go to you to keep or to sell. Whatever you want.'

'Please don't talk about such horrible things.'

'What? Acres in Scotland?'

'No! About … you know… something happening to you.'

'Ellie, darling, we have to face facts that my time will come and then you need to know that this café will be yours. And the cottage, too.'

'Gran!' Ellie took a gulp of tea to ease her aching throat. The thought of a world without Pearl Draper around was far too awful to contemplate.

'Your mum knows that you're my sole beneficiary and she's happy with that. Should you wish to stay on in Cornwall, you'll have this place and the cottage to call home. Or to sell, but that will be your choice.'

'I'd rather keep you forever.'

Her gran laughed. 'Well, you have me for now. And we need to get some baking done for the day ahead and to get planning because there are spring events to organise.'

'Yes, Gran!' Ellie slid off the stool and took their mugs to the sink.

Outside the window, the shadows were moving across the garden as the sun rose in the sky and she could see the chickens and the rooster trotting around in the run. She'd go out and check for fresh eggs in a bit and then help her gran with the baking and other food preparation. With it being Saturday, it would be busy and she was looking forward to another day of serving the villagers. She hoped that Jasper would also come to the café that day; if she had the chance, she would try to think of something interesting to say to him so he wouldn't think her conversation was limited to food, coffee, and the weather.

She could do that, couldn't she?

13
JASPER

When Jasper asked his children what they wanted to do Saturday morning, and they replied that they wanted to walk the dog on the beach and then have breakfast at the café, he was secretly delighted. Granted, he had been there a bit more often in the past fortnight than normal, but he'd told himself it was good to get out and work somewhere else. His daily routine had still involved taking the children to school, walking Wiggy and sorting some chores before school pickup, but being able to head to the café and have a coffee and an almond croissant or a bacon roll was something to look forward to. He told himself it was because it broke up his day and that had to be good for his mental health, but he knew there was more to it. He liked seeing Ellie's lovely smile. Had he not known her, he wouldn't have been surprised to discover she was Pearl's granddaughter. The kindness and warmth must run through the family as they were both very easy to be around. Of course, there was no denying that Ellie was a very beautiful woman, but for Jasper, that wasn't relevant. He wasn't interested in getting to know her because of that, but because of how he felt when he was around her. He was also curious about why she'd suddenly returned to the village and if she would stay there. They hadn't even had a proper conversation yet, but Jasper had found that he became shy in her presence, a bit like an awkward teenager who couldn't speak to girls. But in this case, he was a grown man, and he was struggling to speak to a woman without blushing or stuttering. He hadn't experienced that in a very long time, not since he first met Kimberley and was overwhelmed by her beauty and intelligence. It had taken him by surprise how much he'd fallen for her back then and he'd known she was the woman he wanted to spend his life with. But now ... He was a single dad with two young children heading to The Garden Café for some Saturday morning breakfast and looking forward to seeing the lovely young woman who worked there.

'Come on then,' he said to Mabel and Alfie as he pushed open the door of the café and held it for them.

The children saw that their favourite table was free, so they went to sit down. Jasper went to the counter to order what they'd requested during their walk there. He waited while the woman in front of him was served, then smiled at Pearl.

'Morning, Jasper.' Pearl was wearing a pink bandana tied around her head so that her hair was held back from her face apart from a few strands that curled over her forehead. Her hazel eyes scanned Jasper's face in the way that always made him feel seen.

'Morning, Pearl.'

'And how are you this fine morning?' she asked.

'It's lovely out. We've had a walk to blow off the cobwebs and dropped Wiggy at home before heading over here.'

'It's such a beautiful spring day, isn't it?' Pearl looked over at the front of the café where the large windows made the most of the view of the gardens.

'It's lovely now that spring has arrived. That felt like a long winter.' He shuddered without meaning to.

'Sometimes the winter can seem to last forever.' She nodded thoughtfully. 'But spring will always return. I've been around for a long time and that's something I've learnt along the way. Whatever happens and however long it feels cold, you'll always feel the warmth of the sunlight on your face again.'

She held his gaze, and he wondered if she was still talking about the weather and the seasons or if there was a deeper meaning behind her words.

'I hope so, Pearl,' he said. For him, it had been a long winter. A three-year-long winter in fact and in previous springs, he'd tried to feel alive and to appreciate the beauty around him, but he hadn't always been able to be present enough. This year, though, for the first time, he felt like he was emerging from winter and wondered if there was a chance that he was starting to heal. That thought was both comforting and terrifying because he felt guilty about the idea of being able to move on and heal when his beautiful wife was no longer there.

'It's OK, Jasper. It's OK to savour the sunlight and the feel of the wind in your hair, to enjoy coffee and your favourite foods. And I don't mean just putting the latter in your mouth in some sort of reflex action, I mean really savouring them. Grief steals so much from us. For a long time after I lost my husband, I couldn't enjoy anything. Except for being with Ellie and that was because it was impossible not to feel alive around that child. But I could barely eat. I walked around like a zombie and just went through the motions. Then, one day, about eighteen months after he'd gone, I was walking along the beach and I had the urge to go for a dip. So I did. It was only April and still quite cold some days, but I stripped down to my undies and ran straight in.'

'You didn't!' Jasper laughed, the thought of Pearl almost skinny dipping on the public beach hilarious. How could she be so brave?

'I wanted to feel alive. And there's nothing like bloody cold water to do exactly that. When I emerged from the sea, I was red all over and shaking like a leaf but I felt alive, I can tell you that much.'

Ellie appeared behind Pearl and stopped to listen. 'Are you telling the story about swimming in your underwear, Gran?' she asked, a smile playing across her pretty lips.

'I am, darling. It was a turning point for me. I couldn't keep going the way I had been, and it was time for me to move forwards. My husband wouldn't have wanted me to wither away but to grab life with both hands and extract every ounce of joy from being here while I could.' She tilted her head, then nodded. 'Sorry, Jasper, you'll have to excuse me. I just heard a timer going off—'

'Gran, there's nothing in the oven.' Ellie frowned.

'Back in a mo!' Pearl dashed into the kitchen, leaving Jasper alone with Ellie.

'Sorry about that.' She worried her full bottom lip. 'Gran tells it like it is, doesn't she?'

'I like how direct she can be and how she's not afraid to talk about things. Lots of people are and it's easier when they're open.'

'I find that, too. I hate trying to guess where I am with people.' She smiled and a faint blush appeared in her cheeks. It made her eyes seem even greener and Jasper thought of rolling hills and summer fields, of picnics in parks with strawberries and champagne and snoozing on blankets under trees.

He shook himself. *What the hell was that?*

'What can I get you?' Ellie asked.

Jasper was in the middle of giving her his order when he felt a tugging at the sleeve of his jumper.

'Daddy!' It was Alfie.

'Yes?'

'Daddy, can I go and visit the chickens? I want to see Chris Hensworth and hear him crowing.'

'Alfie, don't forget what we talked about. When Daddy is speaking to someone, try not to interrupt.'

'Sorry, Daddy!' Alfie put a small hand over his mouth, then removed it. 'I am very sorry.'

'We're going to have breakfast first and then maybe you can see the chickens before we leave.' He looked up at Ellie who was smiling at Alfie.

'You certainly can go and see them. I could take you if you like?'

'No, it's fine. You're working and…' Jasper leant over the counter, then whispered, 'I worry if you took him out now you wouldn't get him back inside. And you're busy, anyway.'

'No problem.' Ellie grinned, exposing small straight white

teeth. Could she be any cuter? 'Perhaps later, then,' she said to Alfie who nodded excitedly.

'I asked Daddy to get a cockerel so it would crow and crow and tell us when it's time to get up.'

'They crow all the time though, Alfie, not just when it's morning,' Jasper said and Ellie giggled.

'They do,' Ellie agreed. 'They can be quite noisy and annoy your neighbours, so it's best to only have a cockerel if you have the room for it. But you are welcome here anytime to visit Chris Hensworth.'

'Thank you, Ellie,' Alfie said.

'It's no problem.' She turned to get their drinks and Jasper leant over and said to Alfie, 'Go sit with Mabel and I'll be over in a minute.'

'Yes, Daddy.'

He watched his son walk over to the table and sit on the sofa next to his sister then she reached over and tickled him under the chin. He scrunched up his face and laughed, so she did it again and Jasper sighed. Now they'd get all hot and bothered and he'd have to calm them down enough to eat their breakfast.

'They're so cute,' Ellie said when he turned back to the counter.

'Thanks. They're wonderful, but they can be … a-a handful.' He gave a small laugh. 'I love them to bits, but they do test my patience some days. I take a lot of deep breaths. Single parenting can be challenging.'

'I can only imagine.' Ellie looked over at the children again and then met Jasper's gaze. 'It's amazing how you manage.'

Her eyes widened, and she shook her head. 'I'm so sorry. That came out wrong and sounded patronising. I didn't mean it like that. What I meant was that being a parent must be hard, so being a single parent, well … you've got to do it all alone. It wasn't because you're a man and I don't think men can manage as well as women. Of course not! I—' She placed her hands on her flaming cheeks and sighed. 'Jasper… I'm sorry … I do this when I'm nervous. I'm babbling and I say things that can come across wrong and…' She smiled. 'I think you're a great dad.'

'Thanks. And I wasn't at all offended. I understand what you're saying. It is hard whatever your gender and some days I get downright exhausted. When Kimberley first passed away, I had help from my parents, but then they had to go home and I had to learn how to manage alone. I find that a routine helps me stay organised, as does the fact that the children are amazing. They look out for each other even though they're so young and they listen to me … most of the time.'

'They're very polite and sweet and it's a pleasure to have them in the café.'

'Thank you.' He got his wallet out of his pocket and paid for his order.

'Where's Wiggy today?' she asked, peering over the counter as if expecting to see him at Jasper's side.

'Oh he's at home. We walked him, then took him home and washed the sand off. He was snoring in a pool of sunlight in front of the bifold doors when we left.'

'It's a good name, Wiggy.'

'It's actually short for Wigglebutt.'

'Wigglebutt!' Ellie threw back her head and laughed, and her face lit up. 'I love it!'

'His butt just wiggles and wiggles.' Jasper shrugged.

'It's brilliant and I can totally see what you mean.' She looked behind him and Jasper turned to see another customer.

'I'd better let you get back to work,' he said.

'When you've finished your breakfasts, give me a shout and I'll come around the back to see the chickens with you. I like making a fuss of them too. They're such friendly little things.'

'That would be great.' Jasper carried the tray of drinks over the table and put it down. His heart was beating faster than usual and he found he was smiling to himself.

'What are you smiling about, Daddy?' Mabel asked.

'Me?'

'Yes, I don't have another daddy, silly,' she said.

'Don't be cheeky.' He shook his head, but he was still smiling. 'And I'm smiling because I'm happy.'

'That's good, Daddy,' she said. 'I like it when you're happy.'

'Me too,' Jasper said, realising that it was true.

'Can we go and see the chickens?' Alfie asked, his earlier request not forgotten. His fascination with the birds meant that most visits to the café included a walk around the gardens to see them. Mabel liked them, but she also enjoyed taking seed for the squirrels and the wild birds that visited the gardens.

'Yes, we can, but first ... breakfast!' Jasper said as he sat down opposite his children.

'We should bring Wiggy next time,' Alfie said. 'He likes the chickens.'

'Perhaps.' Jasper nodded.

Because dogs were allowed inside, Jasper sometimes brought Wiggy to the café. However, Wiggy tended to get incredibly excited when he spotted a squirrel. If he saw one before they went in, he would press his nose against the window, panting and smearing the glass as he scanned the gardens. And when he spotted a squirrel… it always led to chaos because he'd start to whimper and scratch at the door, desperate to get outside and give chase. So, this morning, Wiggy had been walked on the beach, had a paddle in the sea then been taken home for a snooze while Jasper and the children went for what he hoped would be a relaxing breakfast.

While they ate, Jasper thought about what Pearl and Ellie had said. It was good to be around people and it was good to talk. He realised he was feeling happy. Not just marginally so, but very much so. It might only be temporary, but it was there. He would try to hold the feeling in his heart because despite the sadness, the grief and the awareness of what he had lost, the happiness glowed there like a candle in the dark.

14
ELLIE

When Jasper and his children had finished their breakfast, he brought the mugs and plates to the counter.

'You don't need to keep doing this,' Ellie said. 'One of us will collect them afterwards.'

He gave a small shrug. 'I can't leave them there. It feels rude.'

'You're a paying customer.'

'But I have manners and I don't like to create more work for you.' He held her gaze, and a small shiver ran down her spine. His blue eyes were so bright and clear and his beard was a rich gold, making her think of pictures she'd seen of Vikings and lumberjacks. With his height and broad shoulders, he could have been either.

'Well, thank you.' She was about to turn away when she remembered Alfie's request. 'Did you want to feed the chickens now?'

Jasper rubbed the back of his neck and smiled. 'Only if you have time. I mean … I can take them around to the chicken run.'

'It's no problem at all. I'll get the food and meet you at the back door.'

'Great.' He nodded, then went back to his children.

Ellie told her gran what she was doing, then went to the kitchen and got some mixed greens and blueberries, then swapped her shoes for wellies in the utility room. By the time she let herself out of the back door, Jasper, Mabel and Alfie were waiting for her.

'What are we giving them?' Alfie asked excitedly.

'These.' She showed him the bowl of greens and berries and he clapped his hands.

'Will they love them?'

'I'm sure they will.' She led the way across the grass and when they reached the chicken run, she unlocked the gate, then turned to Jasper and his children.

'Do you want to come inside?' she asked.

'No, thank you.' Mabel shook her head and looked down at her pink trainers.

'Oh!' Ellie said. 'I could have got you some wellies.'

'I'm OK to watch from here.' Mabel smiled sweetly, toying with one of her dark plaits.

'I want to come inside!' Alfie bobbed from one foot to the other.

'*Please*.' Jasper ruffled his son's blond hair.

Alfie stepped closer to Ellie. 'Please, may I come with you?'

Ellie's heart squeezed. 'Of course you can. Are your shoes going to be OK, though?' She glanced at Jasper and he nodded.

'It's fine. The walk home will clean anything off them.'

'There's a tap near the back door of the café so we can wash them there.' Ellie gestured towards the café.

'Right then … If I hold the bowl, you can scatter the greens and blueberries for the hens. They will get quite excited, so watch your fingers and take care not to trip over any of them.'

'OK. I will be careful.' Alfie looked at her with his blue eyes so similar to his dad's, and she thought he was utterly adorable.

Ellie let them into the run and closed the gate behind her, then she crouched down so Alfie could reach into the bowl. He scattered the food around and the chickens came running, clucking happily and tucking in. Alfie giggled with joy, and Ellie watched as his smile broadened. At one point, she looked up to see Jasper gazing at them with an expression on his face that she couldn't read. It made her curious to know what he was thinking and if he was all right. He'd been through a lot and was raising his beautiful children alone, so he had a lot of responsibility on his shoulders. Ellie knew he was older than her but not by how much, although she knew the children were seven and five, so he'd probably been around her age when Mabel was born. She found it hard to imagine having children at the age of twenty-eight, although she knew many did when they were younger than her. But then her life had been different to some, and she'd often felt like she was just starting out. It was probably due to the insecurity of not having a job that paid a living wage — the bar work had been poorly paid and a zero-hours contract — and to the way she had lived with Barnaby. There had been no sign of a commitment between them or of finding their own place and so she'd lived day to day without allowing herself to think too far ahead. But if you had children like Jasper, you'd have to consider how every decision would affect not just you but your children. Was she capable of making such an adjustment in her life? Possibly, given the right partner and circumstances. But what were the chances of that happening, anyway? She liked Jasper and his children, but he'd given her no sign that he even fancied her. And here she was, letting her imagination run away with her. Jasper was a single dad, and she was a jobless actor living in her childhood home with her gran without a clue about what came next.

And yet, when she smiled at Jasper from her position inside the chicken run, and Jasper smiled back, she felt sure there was a connection growing between them. Call it an overactive imagination, but she'd never looked into another person's eyes and felt this kind of draw before. There was something very special about Jasper Holmes, and Ellie wanted to get to know him better. Whether he felt the same was something she had yet to discover.

15

JASPER

Watching Ellie with Alfie as they fed the chickens and her patience in repeating their names several times because Alfie found it so funny, Jasper felt strange. He wasn't quite sure what it was, but Ellie was so kind and patient with Alfie and he could see that his son liked her. Children were usually pretty good judges of character and Alfie was, at just five years old, apt to speak his mind. Jasper encouraged politeness in his children, but there was no changing the fact that children could be brutally honest. Alfie was no exception. When they emerged from the chicken run, Ellie got Alfie to help her lock it, then she took him to swill his trainers under the tap.

Unlike her brother, Mabel had stuck close to Jasper's side, holding his hand and leaning against him. She was a friendly child, but she had quiet moments when he worried about how serious she could be. Her mum had been the same and had times when she'd seemed lost in her thoughts, but it had been something Jasper was used to. It had meant that Kimberley was mulling something over, whether work or life related, and he knew she'd work it through, then speak to him about it. With such a responsible job, she had reason to need quiet times, and he'd never pressured her to tell him what was on her mind but waited until she was ready. It was one reason why they had worked so well; they understood each other. But as far as Mabel was concerned, she was very young. Jasper worried she could be missing her mum and afraid of losing him too, so he did his best to encourage her to speak to him so he could allay any fears she might have. Of course, the hardest thing about that was that he could never reassure her enough. How could he promise he'd always be there for her when her mum had been ripped away from her so suddenly? The reality of losing a parent the way his children had was that they knew all too well that when someone died, they wouldn't be coming back. Alfie had been younger and so he had limited memories of his mum, but Mabel remembered more about what it had been like to have Kimberley around. Some days, Jasper struggled to navigate the difficult situation, and felt overwhelmed, but he made an effort to stay calm and composed for the sake of the children, portraying a serene facade despite the chaos within.

Suddenly, it hit Jasper how lonely he was. Not having another adult around was hard, and now that he seemed to be emerging from the fog that had enveloped him for the past three years, the loneliness was suddenly very raw. How long had it been since another adult had hugged him? His parents didn't count, although he knew they'd been trying to give him space because they tended to suffocate him with their worrying sometimes.

Alfie shook his trainers off, then ran over and hugged Jasper's legs while babbling on about how much fun he'd had, and Jasper pushed his thoughts aside.

'Thanks so much for that,' he said to Ellie.

'It was my pleasure.' She reached up and pushed a few strands of long black hair that had escaped the claw clip behind her ears. 'You can come and help me feed the hens whenever you like.'

'Thank you, Ellie.' Alfie grinned at her. 'Are we going home now to see Wiggy?'

'In a bit, yes.' Jasper nodded.

'Right, I'd better get back inside.' Ellie picked up the bowl that had contained the greens and berries and tucked it under her arm. She'd swilled it out under the tap after she'd helped Alfie with his shoes.

'See you soon.' Jasper said. 'Probably in the week.'

'Yes. You most likely will!' She gave a small wave then turned and opened the back door of the café before disappearing inside.

'Daddy, can we walk around the gardens before we go home, please?' Mabel asked.

'Of course we can.'

While the children skipped around the gardens, Jasper took advantage of the opportunity to clear his head. The Garden Café was nestled in beautiful gardens not far from the cliffs overlooking the stunning sandy cove. When you walked to the highest point of the gardens, you could see over the hedge and gaze at the shimmering expanse of sea and rocky outcrops, and watch boats bobbing on the horizon. With spring came bursts of colour from the tulips, crocuses, primroses, and daffodils, the varying purples of the different types of lavender, and buds on trees and rosebushes. Herbs grew in raised beds, and Jasper couldn't resist running his hands over the rosemary bushes and inhaling their sharp, refreshing scent. All around the gardens, trees unfurled their fresh green leaves and there was a sense of hope and renewal in the air. As Jasper walked, he could feel it in his bones, and again he had that sense of awakening after a long, cold winter. There was life in him yet and maybe, just maybe, there was the possibility of finding a connection with another person again. Maybe he could find love again. Or was one love enough for a lifetime? He was still young and his children were young and he could choose to spend the rest of his life alone or he could embrace this spring and give himself permission to open his heart.

He took a deep cleansing breath, then called his children. 'Come on, you two, I have something I need to do.'

'What is it, Daddy?' Mabel asked, taking his right hand while Alfie took the left.

'Let's head down to the beach and I'll show you.'

Twenty minutes later, after giving Alfie a piggyback and holding tight to Mabel's hand, Jasper was walking across the sand of the beach. He set Alfie down and looked out at the sea. In the spring sunlight, the water looked bright blue and rather cold. But he had made up his mind, and he was going to go for it.

He crouched down and took his children's hands. 'Do you two know how much I love you?'

'Yes, Daddy.' Mabel said.

'Yes!' Alfie giggled, wondering at this new game.

'You are my world. I always want you to remember that. Your mum was a wonderful person and she loved you both very much. You were everything to her.'

'What's wrong, Daddy?' Mabel's eyes filled with apprehension.

'Well, you know how I'm always pretty sensible and calm and… Daddy-like?'

They both nodded.

'Sometimes, I want to do something a bit … different.'

'Like what?' Alfie asked, eyes wide.

'A friend of mine told me recently that she went for a dip in the sea one day. She didn't have her swimming costume, so she just went in anyway.'

'That's funny, Daddy!' Mabel laughed.

'You guys fancy a paddle?' he asked.

'It will be cold.' Mabel shivered. 'It was freezing when we walked Wiggy earlier.'

'I do!' Alfie was always up for doing something daring.

'Oh me too, then.' Not to be outdone by her brother, Mabel removed her trainers and socks and rolled up her trousers.

They put their trainers and socks in a pile, then Jasper sucked in a breath and removed his jacket, jumper and T-shirt.

'What are you doing?' Mabel shrieked. 'You don't need to undress to paddle.'

'I'm going to have a quick dip in the water.' Jasper's skin pebbled with goosebumps. It might be spring but it was still incredibly fresh. He looked down at his jeans and realised he couldn't get them wet, so he whipped them off too and stood there in his boxers (that were luckily black and baggy) then he turned to the water again. 'OK. Now don't worry because I'm not going mad, but I need to have a quick dip in the sea. You two wait at the shoreline for me and I'll be super fast.'

They jogged down to the water, both children chuckling at the craziness of the moment.

'I'll be in and out.' Jasper kissed them both on the head, then let go of their hands. He noticed with a tugging at his heartstrings how Mabel took hold of her brother's hand and stood with him. 'Here goes!'

He gritted his teeth, submerging himself to his waist. The shock of the cold bit into his skin and his breath caught in his throat, but there was no going back now. He had to keep going forwards. It was, he thought, like a metaphor for life. You couldn't turn back time or change the past. Instead, you had to keep going, even if sometimes reluctantly.

'Go on, Daddy! You can do it!' He turned and saw Mabel waving her free hand above her head like a cheerleader with an invisible pompom.

'Go on, Daddy!' Alfie echoed his sister's encouragement.

'OK!' He blew them kisses. 'Here goes!'

He sucked in a breath, then plunged beneath the water. Cold enveloped him and water filled his ears, covered his head, embraced him like an ardent lover. He opened his eyes and peered out at his surroundings, seeing endless blue-green, the sand beneath his feet and some seaweed floating past. It was quiet, all sound muffled, and he took a moment to savour the peace but then his lungs needed emptying, so he rose to the surface and burst from the water.

The first thing he saw was his children waiting on the shore and then, over near the cliffs, another figure. Gazing his way. He blinked to clear the salt water from his eyes, but it stung so he rubbed them. When he could see again, he looked over to the cliffs, but the figure was gone as if she'd disappeared into thin air.

Which she had.

If she'd ever been there at all.

He turned back to his children and waded out of the water to them, then he took their hands and squeezed them.

'How was it?' Mabel asked.

'F-freezing!' He laughed then looked down at himself. 'I don't suppose either of you has a towel in your pocket, do you?'

'I have a packet of tissues.' Mabel said, offering it to him.

'Thanks.' He accepted the packet and when they got to their belongings, he pulled a tissue out and started trying to pat himself dry.

While Mabel and Alfie put their trainers on, Jasper's eyes strayed to the cliffs again. When he'd emerged from the water, he'd been sure he'd seen her. *Kimberley*. Smiling and waving and looking exactly as she had that last day when she'd left for work. Was it simply muscle memory? His brain trying to make sense of what had happened and what he'd lost? Was it the cleansing effect of the icy water on his skin as it washed away the past, renewing him from the outside in? Or had Kimberley come to show him she approved of what he was doing, of the fact that he was finally allowing himself to heal and to let go of the guilt. He knew deep down that she would never want him to feel guilty about her death, but being left behind when she'd been taken away and in such a horrid manner had left him feeling more guilt than he could process. And so it had been something he'd needed to work through, one day, one hour, one minute at a time. That was all people could do with grief because the thought of how they'd manage without a loved one for the rest of their days was enough to break their heart and minds.

One day at a time ... His mum had said the words to him and so had Pearl. There was much wisdom in that approach to getting through the grieving process.

He slid his left leg into his jeans, then his right, pulling them up; his face contorting into a grimace as they clung to his wet boxers. When they got home he'd have a hot shower and put some warm clothes on. He didn't even mind the discomfort for now because his dip in the sea had done exactly what he'd wanted. As soon as Pearl had told him she'd done it, he'd known he needed to do it too and now he did feel different. Refreshed. Renewed. Ready to make some changes. And he hoped seeing him do it would be good for his children. They needed to know that he was human too, not invincible, not without emotion, not set in his ways. He was their dependable Daddy, yes, but he could also be fun. And occasionally unpredictable. Had Pearl had other motives for telling him the story then? Had she known that he would copy what she had done and experience the same sense of renewal?

After he had put on all his clothes, he took hold of his children's hands.

'I don't know about you two, but I feel hungry again.'

'Probably all the calories you burnt off in the cold water, Daddy,' Mabel said, sounding like a teenager and not the child she was. There was no doubt that she was her mother's daughter, no doubt at all.

'I'm hungry!' Alfie said. 'Can we have chips?'

'Chips, eh?' Jasper thought about freshly cooked chips covered in salt and vinegar. 'Chips it is! Let's go get some.'

Mabel and Alfie cheered, then they walked up from the beach and into the village. Jasper looked around him, seeing everything as if for the first time. He had been to the depths of despair, but now, hopefully, he could rise again.

16
ELLIE

Saturday at the café had been busy. Her gran only opened the café on Sundays during the summer months, from June to August, and sometimes through the rest of the year on special occasions. On the Sunday just gone, Ellie and her gran went for a lovely beach walk before enjoying a roast dinner that they cooked together. They'd had a very chilled day, and it had set them up for the week. Ellie was still getting stuck in at the café and her gran had insisted that she would start paying her now, because she needed an income. Ellie had tried to resist, but her gran had recently lost an employee who'd moved away from the village, so she said it was useful to have Ellie there. Plus, she'd added, she wanted Ellie to work there so she could decide if it was what she'd want to do long-term, either when she inherited the café or took over from Pearl. As always, Pearl insisted there was no pressure and Ellie loved her for it.

Wednesday had dawned as perfectly as most days had since Ellie's return, with a beautiful sunrise and a crisp, cloudless sky. As March progressed, it was getting warmer (if only slightly) and signs of spring were evident everywhere. Ellie enjoyed taking her breaks in the café gardens where she would find a quiet spot and sit on one of the rustic wooden benches under the mature trees. There, she'd listen to the birdsong, trying to decipher what birds she could hear in the way her grampa had taught her. The one bench was at the highest point of the garden and it was possible to sit there and gaze out to sea. It was a wonderful place to relax and more than once, Ellie had dozed off as she listened to the birds and, when the wind was blowing briskly, the sound of the sea. At those times, she could also smell the salt on the air and it was fresh and uplifting, so different to the air in London. She loved London for being so vibrant and busy, but for her, now she was home, she knew Cornwall would always have her heart. There was no beating the smell of the sea, the peace of watching boats sailing across the horizon, and the sense of peace she found being back in the village. Once upon a time, she would have scoffed at the idea of settling down there, but now, she realised that living there could well be the route to happiness and contentment for her.

And, of course, there was Jasper. She couldn't deny the impact of seeing him on an almost daily basis and learning more about him and his young family. He wasn't much older than Barnaby. She'd found out this week that he was thirty-five, but he seemed so mature while Barnaby had, in retrospect, been like a spoilt child. She had yet to hear from him how his travels were going, although she really wasn't bothered if she did. It felt strange to transition from living together to complete indifference towards his presence, but she now realised their relationship had continued purely out of habit, and being apart from him had helped her see that. She suspected that some part of her would always care for

Barnaby because they had been together for some time, but not enough to want to be with him in a relationship. Besides which, she knew now that he didn't care about her and what was the point of being in a one-sided relationship with someone? It had been all give on her part and all take on his. She didn't blame Barnaby entirely for that as his parents had nurtured that selfishness in him, but he should take some responsibility for it because he was an adult. She could only hope that his travels would open his eyes to what others went through and that he would return to London a changed man. Hope, that was, but not expect, because it was possible Barnaby would not change and that he would continue to be the man she'd known. It was no longer her problem though, and so she wished him well.

This evening, she was looking forward to yoga in the café gardens. Her gran was a qualified yoga teacher, and she held classes in the gardens during warmer weather. This evening was the first class of the year.

After they'd cleaned the kitchen, she changed into her sports gear in the staff toilets and looked down at herself. She was wearing the clothes she'd worn for her audition that seemed such a long time ago. How could it be only five and a half weeks since she'd stood on that stage and watched her pump hit the casting director? It felt like years and that was the benefit of coming home to Cornwall. She had put distance between herself and the life she'd led in London, and she felt very different. Far more like herself. It made her aware of exactly how much she'd been trying to force herself to be a certain way in London, to fit the mould that Barnaby, his parents, and Ramona wanted her to fit. But as with trying to fit a square peg into a round hole, it didn't work and Ellie could now see that. Time and space were incredibly beneficial when trying to work out what she wanted to do and what she wanted from her life. She'd started to understand that having a family was something she could want. Seeing Jasper and his children, as well as other families around the village had confirmed this for her. The time she spent with little Mabel and Alfie when they came to the café made her so happy. She had even joined them in the café the previous evening and read to them while Jasper had taken an important work call on his mobile outside. He'd been very apologetic, but she'd enjoyed herself. She'd also liked the fact that he trusted her with his children, even if he had only been outside and could still see them all. While Jasper had been on the call, Alfie had told Ellie that after they'd left the café on Saturday, his daddy had gone into the sea in just his boxers. Ellie had thought he was joking, but Mabel had confirmed it. The children had giggled as if it was the funniest thing ever. Alfie had then told her they'd had chips and sausage from the chip shop and it had been the best dinner he'd ever had. Ellie admitted she loved chip shop chips and Alfie had invited her to dinner with them one day soon so she could have chips with lots of salt and vinegar like their daddy.

When Ellie walked back out into the café, her gran whistled. 'Look at you, sexy pants!'

'What?' Ellie laughed.

'In your yoga gear.'

'It's actually clothing I bought for auditions, but it's perfect for yoga.'

Her gran had taught her yoga routines when she was a child and they'd often done it together, but Ellie had been so busy she hadn't bothered for a while. 'I think I'm going to be quite stiff this evening, so please don't laugh at me.'

'Ellie, yoga isn't about mocking people, it's about getting in touch with your body and your breath. It's about doing what's comfortable for you and increasing flexibility. It will do you good. And this evening's yoga has a special surprise.'

'Does it? What is it?'

'It wouldn't be a surprise if I told you now, would it?' Her gran laughed, then opened the door. 'Come along then, let's get everything set up before people arrive.'

A blackbird's song and the mellow strumming of a harp filled the evening air. When they reached the area of the gardens where yoga took place, Ellie smiled to see a local woman sitting on a stool with her harp in front of her.

'Hello, Cariad.' Her gran placed a hand on the woman's shoulder.

'Hello there.' Cariad Jones smiled. 'It's a beautiful evening for it.'

'Indeed it is.' Ellie's gran went to the storage shed that was disguised by the net of faux leaves draped over it. She unlocked it and pulled out a large basket filled with yoga mats. Ellie went to help her and they started setting the mats out in a semi-circle with Pearl's mat at the core.

'Was that the surprise?' Ellie asked, nodding at Cariad.

'Oh no, darling. There's more.' Her gran chuckled.

People started arriving and taking the mats and Ellie wandered around greeting them. She went back to the café to get the basket of drinks they'd prepared earlier and was just leaving the café when she paused. Her heart skipped a beat. Because there was Jasper, wearing joggers and a fitted T-shirt as he walked up the path to the café. Was he coming to yoga too? And if so, where were the children? It was almost 7pm, so he would normally have been getting them ready for bed, surely?

He spotted her and waved, then jogged over to her.

'Here, let me take that for you.' He reached for the basket and she was about to decline, but then she decided to let him help.

'Thanks. It's nice to see you here.'

'I've wanted to try Pearl's yoga classes for a while, but it's difficult with the children. I know this is the first one this year and didn't think I'd be able to come, but my parents turned up this afternoon, unexpectedly, so they're babysitting.'

'How lovely!' Ellie said, feeling very pleased to see him. 'Are you OK?'

He nibbled at his bottom lip. 'Why do you ask?'

'Well ... I know it must be hard for you to leave them at all.'

He gave a wry laugh. 'You're not wrong there, but my parents are great with them and said I should have an evening off.'

'They don't live locally then?'

He shook his head. 'They live in Oxford, where I'm from. It's a long journey, so they try to fit in some other visits along the way. They're here for two nights then visiting friends in Devon.'

He frowned. 'Are your parents local?'

Ellie inhaled slowly. 'My Mum lives in Scotland. She moved there a long time ago. As for my dad ... I have no idea.'

'No?' Jasper's frown deepened.

'He left when I was six. I was basically raised by my gran and grampa. My mum was around but after my gramps passed away when I was eight, my mum didn't cope very well. She then met her second husband on a dating app and moved to Scotland to be with him. He's truly lovely and adores her.'

'But you didn't go with her?' There was a gentle curiosity in his eyes, and Ellie found that she didn't mind telling him about her past. It wasn't always easy to explain to people, but she got the feeling Jasper wouldn't judge her, but he would be concerned for her feelings.

'No, I stayed here with Gran. I couldn't bear to leave her as she's always been more of a mum to me, anyway.'

'Pearl is a special lady.' Jasper smiled.

'That's very true.' Ellie glanced around. 'We'd probably better get a move on or there won't be any mats left.'

'I know!' He grinned. 'Come on, then.'

Jasper set the basket down near Pearl, then he took a mat at the outside of the semi-circle. Ellie took one on the opposite side and sat down with her legs crossed.

Her gran talked them through some stretches and a gentle warm up and Ellie felt herself relaxing. The harp filled the air with a beautiful tune. The scent of magnolia and lavender washed over her and her gran's calming voice led her through the sequence.

She was drifting off in savasana when she felt something tickle her right cheek. She brushed her hand absently at it, but it happened again, so she opened her eyes and sat up.

'Oh my goodness!' She squealed as others around her did, too. Puppies cavorted among them, leaping onto mats, slobbering on faces, nipping toes, and scrambling over people. Her gran was sitting on her mat with a puppy on her lap, cradling it like a baby.

'Sorry for the surprise!' her gran said. 'But I thought it would be a good way to introduce you to some of the puppy residents from the local dog sanctuary. These cuties are all looking for their forever homes. My friend, Leanne Penrose, manages the sanctuary and she agreed to come here this evening with the puppies.' She pointed over at a woman standing with two others near the café. 'They are happy to do this to socialise the puppies and to get the message out to the community that these special little ones are available for adoption.'

Ellie looked over at Jasper and saw that he had a small black and white dog that looked like a collie mix trying to nibble at his ear. Jasper was laughing and it seemed to make the puppy try even harder.

'Just in case anyone is wondering, they've all had their vaccines so aren't at risk being out and about.' Pearl bobbed her head in Leanne's direction and the other woman smiled. 'Right then, shall we continue with our class?'

Ellie had to admit that the class had started off very relaxing, but with the puppies involved, it was significantly less so. However, it was certainly not less enjoyable. Leanne and her colleagues occasionally had to round up puppies that were wandering off and then they plonked them back with the yoga class, which the puppies seemed to enjoy. There was a lot of nibbling and tugging of hair and clothes, and Ellie laughed so much her stomach ached by the end of the hour.

When the puppies had said their goodbyes and Leanne had taken them back to the sanctuary, Ellie put the mats away and Jasper gave them a hand. He really was very considerate, and it made her like him even more.

'I'm going to speak to Cariad for a bit and hang around for a coffee,' her gran said, glancing at Jasper. 'Why don't you head home and I'll meet you there?'

'Sure.' Ellie hugged her gran.

'I'm heading your way, so is it OK if I walk with you?' Jasper asked.

'I'd like that.' Ellie cursed her cheeks for flushing because she suspected it was what her gran had hoped for. 'I'll just grab my things and then we can go.'

Jasper waited on the path for her and when she returned to his side, he offered to take her bag.

'It's fine, honestly. It's not at all heavy.' She hooked the rucksack over her back and tucked her hands into her pockets.

It was colder now, and the moon glowed brightly while the stars twinkled overhead as the sky changed from amber and pink to navy blue.

'Fancy stopping by the beach on the way?' he asked.

'Why not?'

So they walked away from the café, and out onto the road, then headed for the beach. Ellie could already hear the soothing sound of the sea as it caressed the shore and smell the briny air. She was very aware of Jasper's tall, solid presence next to her and how much she liked him, how much she was already starting to care about him. But then her gran had always told her that when you met the one for you, it was just right. From the get-go. There might to seem to be any rhyme or reason to it, but she would know. And whenever she was close to Jasper, Ellie thought she could understand what her gran meant. It had been a long time coming and Barnaby had been a false start but finally, she felt like she was on the right track.

Was it possible that here in Porthpenny, in the village where she had grown up, she had finally met the one?

17
JASPER

Jasper paused outside his front door, needing a moment before he went inside. He'd walked home with Ellie after yoga and his mind was filled with thoughts of how much he liked her, his heart was filled with yearning and he was incredibly confused. The confusion that clouded his thoughts seemed to weigh heavily on his shoulders, causing tension to creep into his muscles. His neck felt stiff and tight. It was as if his body was mirroring the internal battle he was waging between logic and emotion. How could he like Ellie so much when he'd only known her a few weeks? How could he even be thinking like this at all when he still loved his wife?

Instead of going straight inside, he turned and walked to the end of the development, then marched along the coastal path for a bit. Gazing out at the water, he focused on the reflection of the moon on its surface. Silver. Bright. Beautiful. He just needed a few moments to clear his head, and then all would be well.

Yoga had been fun, especially when the puppies had been introduced to the group. He knew that when he got home, though, Wiggy was going to sniff him all over and be furious that his dad had been with another dog and not taken him. He'd thought about taking Wiggy to the local residential home to visit the residents because he knew other people whose dogs were welcome visitors there. Dogs could bring so much joy and he knew Wiggy could brighten his day, so why not that of other people? The main issue with it, as far as he could predict, would be that Wiggy might consume too many treats and put weight on. Chocolate Labs could be notoriously greedy and Wiggy was no exception.

He stopped walking and folded his arms as he looked around him. The coastal path was beautiful even at night, and he knew how lucky he was to be able to access it from his street. Breathing deeply, he felt shivers run down his spine. The past few weeks had been strange and yet wonderful. Like a caterpillar emerging from a cocoon, he was changing. It had been a slow process and at times a frustrating one, but to see the world around him with fresh eyes was amazing. Before he'd lost Kimberley, he'd heard other people talk about grief and how it changed their lives, that it took as long as it took to feel more positive about life again. But he'd seen it as something that happened to other people and not thought it would happen to him. Sure, everyone expected to lose grandparents and parents, but no one expected to lose their partner so young. It just wasn't how things were meant to be. And then there was the permanency of death: once you were gone, there was no coming back. How utterly heart-breaking possessing that knowledge was.

And the guilt ... The guilt was crippling. Not just the survivor guilt that he was still there and his wife was not, that was bad enough, but the guilt that he'd wished to go too.

He'd begged the universe to take him in the days and weeks after he'd lost Kimberley. The thought of trying to live without her, trying to exist without the woman who had filled his heart, mind, and body with vigour and joy had been unbearable. How could he possibly go on without her? He had even considered how he could leave this life to be with her. But then it had hit him over and over like the agony of a broken bone, that if something happened to him, his children, Kimberley's children, would be alone in the world. How dreadful a thought that had been. Yes, his parents would probably have taken the little ones in, but they were ageing, they had their own lives and things they still wanted to do and … He rubbed at his eyes now, shook himself because the darkness was hovering over him like a cloud. If he had gone too, then what would his children have thought? Losing both parents in such a short space of time would have been awful for them.

Whatever happened, Jasper had to be there for his children and to stay strong, fit and healthy for them. He would guide them into adulthood for their sake and for Kimberley's. It was what she would have wanted and even if he had to suffer the pain of his loss on a daily basis, their children would not have to lose him, too.

And now, looking back, he could see the strength he had shown in accepting that he had to be there for Mabel and Alfie. He had kept going for them. It hadn't been easy, and some days had broken him over and over again, but he'd got through and emerged the next day and the day after that. Before he knew it, a year had passed, then another, and now it had been three years and he was still here.

Still living with pain and grief, but they were no longer as sharp. He had grown around the grief as he had come to terms with it, and recently been able to see that there was still a life to be lived. It was a different life and one in which he would always miss Kimberley, but it was a life, nonetheless. He lived for his children. And he lived for Wiggy.

He was, he realised, as he turned and walked home, also glad to be there. People had told him after he'd lost Kimberley that he should reach out and ask for help if he felt it was all too much for him, but he had found that difficult. How could you confess your innermost darkness to others? He'd never been an over-sharer, it just wasn't his style. The thought of telling others that he could barely get out of bed in the morning and that he felt utterly broken wasn't something he was comfortable with. The strange thing about it was that people just seemed to know, even though he hadn't told them. Pearl, for instance, would hold his gaze and communicate her understanding with her eyes in a way that helped. She wasn't able to comfort him by taking away his pain, but being understood had helped, even if just a tiny bit. A hand on his shoulder, a fresh cup of coffee when he was working on his laptop at the café, a kind smile, and a kind word... The power of these things was not to be underestimated. Add to that, a walk on the beach, a swim in the sea, a good meal and, more recently, a beer with friends and Jasper counted himself lucky. He was surrounded by people and things that had helped him to get through the days. Alone, these things didn't seem to make much difference, but like pennies in a jar, they added up. One penny wouldn't make a difference to someone's finances but a jar full would do and it was the same with positive actions. The pennies wouldn't pay off his mortgage just like a walk or a good cup of coffee wouldn't heal his grief, but they would help. Bit by bit, he would heal and grow stronger again.

He let himself into his home and removed his trainers, then crouched down as a sleepy Wiggy came to greet him. Wiggy wagged his lovely tail, then his ears perked up as he smelt the puppies on Jasper. He subjected Jasper to a full sniff search from top to toe, his nose tickling and making him laugh.

'There you are,' his mum said as she descended the stairs. 'We were wondering where you'd got to, Jasper.'

'Sorry … it went on for longer than expected and then I walked home with a friend.'

'A friend?' His mum smiled, her eyes widening slightly as her interest was piqued. He knew she'd love to know more. She'd asked him many times over the past three years to consider dating again. Just to get out there and see that there were other people in the world and other women who could also love him. He'd refused, of course, and he'd seen the sadness in her eyes. Because didn't any loving parent want their child to be happy? To see them love and be loved? His dad had given him a man hug and whispered to him that all he needed to do was to tell his mum he was dating again, even if he wasn't, just to stop her worrying so much. Jasper had felt angry that they were being so insensitive. Didn't they understand how heartbroken he was and how the thought of dating sickened him? How would they have felt if they'd lost each other when their lives were just getting started? How would they have felt if…

But now he could see that they did understand, and they did sympathise and they did love him and want the best for him. Witnessing his heartbreak must have been dreadful for them, and they simply wanted for him to find some joy and some comfort.

'Fancy a cuppa?' he asked.

'That would be lovely.'

They went through to the kitchen and she told him the children had gone to bed like little angels. She'd read them a story, then Jasper's dad had read them a story and tucked them in. No sooner had Jasper's parents come downstairs than they'd heard feet on the landing and tiptoeing down the stairs along with giggling. Jasper's dad had gone to the hallway and scooped the children up, making them giggle harder. He'd taken them back upstairs and read them another story. When Jasper's mum had crept up to check on him half an hour later, he'd been snoring away on Mabel's bed with Mabel and Alfie on either side of him. The book had been open on his lap, his glasses still on his nose and the nightlight projecting a galaxy of stars on the ceiling. Jasper's mum had removed the book and his glasses, covered him and the children with a blanket, turned off the light, and closed the door. There would be no waking him now, she'd said, and Jasper knew she was right. Once his dad went to sleep, an earthquake wouldn't wake him.

Sitting at the kitchen island with mugs of tea in front of them, Jasper's mum said, 'You're not annoyed, are you?'

He met her blue eyes and frowned. 'Why would I be annoyed?'

'Well ... the children were up a bit later than their usual routine and now your dad is sleeping in with them. I know you like to stick to their routines.'

'Mum, I'm not annoyed at all. Routines have helped us all to manage, but Mable and Alfie don't see you and Dad that often and so when you're here, it should be a special time.'

'Thank you.' She pushed her bobbed blond hair behind her ears. It was the same colour as Jasper's but dyed these days because she'd gone white some years ago. She was sixty-four and looked good. She walked and played golf and ate well. But looking at her now, Jasper couldn't deny that time was passing. She had fine lines around her eyes and mouth, there were a few brown patches on her skin and the veins on her hands were more prominent than he remembered. While he'd been lost in his grief, life had been carrying on and his parents had been getting older. He hadn't noticed, had viewed them the same way he always done, but he had to face the fact that time waited for no one. Life moved on and he should make the most of those he loved while they were still around. 'It's so lovely to spend time with you all.'

'Same.' He sipped his tea. 'I'm sorry I haven't said it before, but you're very welcome to visit more often.'

His mum cupped her hands around her mug and licked her lips. 'We … haven't wanted to crowd you. We know how important it is for you to get on with things. After … after Kimberley passed away, we were here a lot, I know, and then that day you said… What you said… and we were so worried we'd been suffocating.' She looked up from her mug and her eyes were glistening. 'All we wanted was to help and to support you, but we were too much and we're both so sorry for that.'

Jasper shook his head. 'No, Mum, it was me who was in the wrong. I shouldn't have snapped like that.'

He had tried not to think about how he'd behaved and what he'd said because beating himself up about it hadn't helped him at all, but he had been in the wrong.

'Jasper, darling, you were consumed with shock and grief. We weren't offended when you told us you needed some space and asked us to stop suffocating you. It was perfectly understandable because we were here *a lot*.'

'I needed you both, but I didn't know how to tell you that. I lost my mind for a while there, Mum.'

'I know, Jasper, and it's not surprising that you did. But never beat yourself up for that because you'd just lost the woman you loved and yet you were holding everything together. You are strong and resilient and you have done incredibly well. We are very proud of you and we love you so much.'

Jasper reached out a hand across the island and his mum squeezed it.

'Thanks, Mum. I love you guys too. It's not always easy for me to tell you. I should be better at it, really. After all, I know all too well that if you don't say something today, then it could be too late tomorrow. I'll try to tell you more often how much you both mean to me.'

'We already know.' His mum's voice was soft, and he held her hand tighter, ran his thumb over the veins and the soft skin that would smell of magnolia hand cream the way it always had. Her hands had smoothed his fevered brow when he'd been unwell as a child, had cleaned up cuts and stuck plasters to his cut knees when he had fallen. These hands had supported him as he trembled at the funeral, feeling like he would topple over with the agony of his emotions. His mum had been there for him and loved him with her whole heart, and that was what he had needed. He just hadn't always appreciated it as much as he should have done. That would change now and he would do what he could to show her how much he adored her and his dad.

'Yoga was good this evening,' he said, wanting to reassure her that he was feeling better.

'I'm so glad, darling.'

'They had puppies there.'

His mum laughed. 'Which is why Wiggy subjected you to a thorough sniffing when you got back.'

'Yes.' Jasper laughed. 'He would have loved it.'

'I'm sure he would. Perhaps you can take him next time.'

'It's an idea.' Jasper could picture Wiggy roaming around sniffing people, perhaps sticking his nose in someone's bottom when they were doing downward dog or licking their face when they were in savasana. Yes, Wiggy would love yoga.

'And you walked home with a friend?' His mum's voice was calm, but she'd clearly been thinking about what he'd said.

'I did. Her name is Ellie and her gran owns The Garden Café.'

'Oh.' His mum nodded and he could see the smoke coming from her ears as she tried not to combust.

'She's lovely. But she's just a friend.'

'OK.' His mum sipped her tea, eyeing him over the rim of her mug.

'Look … I know that you and dad just want me to be happy and recently I've started to feel a bit better. I will always miss Kimberley and always love her, but I'm … I don't quite know how to put this… I feel like I'm emerging from the darkness. Like I can finally allow myself to feel hope and joy again.'

His mum nodded slowly, her wide eyes glued to his face.

'I've felt like I was … under a cloud, like I couldn't breathe some days, but with time, it has eased. I feel guilty for saying that, like I have no right to feel more positive, but I know Kimberley wouldn't want me to struggle forever.'

'Of course she wouldn't. Kimberley loved you and would want you to embrace your life for your sake and for the children. If it was the other way around, you wouldn't want her to hate life, would you?'

'I'd want her to live.'

'Exactly. And so you must live too.' His mum sighed. 'None of us gets long, Jasper. Some have more time than others, but the years pass so quickly. I'll be sixty-five next birthday and your dad will be sixty-nine. It seems like mere weeks since I was twenty-five. You are a young man and you have so much to live for and so much to offer. I'm not saying that you have to fall in love again, because I know that's complicated for you with the children and your loss, but you could enjoy spending time with someone and see how it goes. A... what is it called? A friend with benefits.'

Jasper laughed. 'I can't believe you just said that, Mum.'

'Nor me!' She giggled.

'You'd like Ellie. She's warm and sweet, she gets on with the children and she makes me smile. But the thing is ... nothing has happened between us. I don't even know if she sees me that way. She's younger than me and probably just sees me as a single dad who has two adorable children and a lot of baggage.'

'But you know there's more to it, don't you?'

'What do you mean?'

'You just know, Jasper. I can see it in your eyes and written all over your face. This woman is special, and she thinks you are too.'

He shook his head. 'I don't know. Maybe my gut is telling me there's something there, but I'm scared, Mum. There's a lot at stake and whatever I want, I can't risk the children getting hurt.'

His mum squeezed his hand again. 'A life lived in fear is no life at all. The children are far stronger than you realise. They are loved and secure and they know it. You are a dad, Jasper, but you are also a man and a human being with a right to love and be loved. Just see how things go. Don't be too hard on yourself and accept things as they happen.'

'Mum?' he asked.

'Yes.'

'Will you and Dad come and visit more often? I've missed you both.'

'Actually, Jasper … we've been thinking about perhaps getting a caravan at the park. Nothing flashy, just something we could stay in so we'd be nearby but not on top of you the way we are when we stay here. That way, we'd be around when you need us and the children could come and sleep over. But only if that was all right with you. There's never any pressure from us. You know that, don't you?'

'I know that, Mum. And I think a caravan is a great idea. The park is open eleven months of the year now.'

His mum nodded. 'We're thinking of selling the house, then we could downsize to the caravan and go abroad when the site is closed.'

'Somewhere with a golf course, I bet!' He laughed.

'You know me so well.'

'Thanks, Mum.'

'What for?'

'For being you.'

'Oh Jasper...' She put her mug down, released his hand and slid off her stool, then she came around the island and stood next to him. 'You're our precious boy. However old you are, you will always be our boy.'

She opened her arms and wrapped them around him, and Jasper settled into her hug. For the first time in a long time, he hugged her back and didn't rush to pull away. His mum understood him far better than he'd realised. There was no judgement or disappointment between them; there was simply love.

18
ELLIE

'What do you think?' Ellie asked as she watched her gran's face carefully.

Sitting at the table closest to the counter in the café kitchen, her gran dabbed at her mouth with a napkin, then reached for her glass of water.

'I think that was delicious!' Her gran rubbed her stomach in the way she'd done when Ellie was a young child to show she'd enjoyed something. 'Absolutely delicious. What's next?'

'Hold on.' Ellie made a quick note on her phone. She'd decided that while she was working at the café, she'd like to be more helpful, and one way of doing that was to help develop the seasonal menu. To create new menu items for the café, she'd scoured websites, cookbooks, and local farm shops for ingredients. She wanted the dishes to be seasonal and locally sourced, organic where possible and different to the usual menu. The first dish she'd served her gran was a spring salad made with radishes, asparagus, and fresh rocket — some ingredients had come from a local farm and some from the raised beds in the café garden. She'd added goat's cheese from the farm and local honey along with a zesty vinaigrette.

It was a beautiful April afternoon; the sunshine streaming through the café windows and warming the space. With it being Sunday, the café was closed to the public, but some people wandered around the gardens that were open throughout the year. Her gran owned the café, but the gardens were owned by the village. Local volunteers tended to the gardens and there was a community fund for plants and seeds. During the warmer months, once things started growing again, there would be plant swaps and food swaps and visits from the local primary school children to teach them about growing fruit and vegetables. Ellie had suggested to her gran that they could hold cooking classes for the children too, and her gran had been very enthusiastic about the idea.

'Right … back soon,' Ellie said as she returned to the kitchen. She added the finishing touches to the next dish then carried it out. 'Here we have wild garlic soup. The garlic was foraged from the garden along with freshly baked bread.'

'It smells incredible,' her gran said.

Ellie looked up then and saw a familiar face smiling through the front window at her. She waved, and he waved back.

'Oh for goodness' sake, Ellie, let the poor man inside.' Her gran tutted before taking another taste of the soup.

At the door, Ellie looked through the glass into Jasper's blue eyes and her heart gave a little flip. She unlocked the door and smiled at him.

'Hello.'

'Hi.' He ran a hand over his golden beard then smiled broadly and Ellie's stomach did a loop the loop. Warmth spread through her body and her skin tingled. The mere sight of his broad smile caused a delicious sensation to travel down her spine. Her cheeks flushed, turning a shade of pink as her pulse quickened. He was always handsome, but when he smiled, it was like the sunshine appearing from behind the clouds. Ellie could feel the heat of his smile all over her skin and it made her want to step forwards and lean against his broad chest. It didn't help that he was wearing a fitted black long-sleeved T-shirt that clung to his muscles, a pair of black shorts over running tights and a black baseball cap that somehow made his eyes look more piercing and his beard more golden. And he was so tall.

'What've you been doing?' she asked, then wanted to kick herself. He had obviously been for a run!

'I went for a run and ended up here.' He glanced behind her at her gran, who waved at him, then pulled out her phone as if she had something important to attend to immediately.

'Oh ... Did you have a nice run?' she asked. Her eyes roamed over his glowing skin and lower where they flickered over his shoulders and sculpted chest. Surely it was criminal for a man to be so attractive?

'I did. I usually run at home on the treadmill because I can't go out when the children are there, although I occasionally go during the day if I have a chance. But there's nothing like running in the fresh air.'

'Would you like to come inside?' she asked. 'I could make you a drink.'

'Won't your gran mind? It is Sunday and I don't want to impose.'

'She won't mind at all.' She paused as something struck her. 'Where are the children?'

'They both had play dates with friends in the village. Their friends are actually siblings, so I dropped them off and will pick them up later.' His brows met for a moment and he pulled his phone from a secret pocket and checked it. 'It's new to me, this letting them out of my sight. I'm trying hard, though. They were desperate to go for this playdate and their friends' parents are great. Trusting others with your children isn't easy, but I know I have to let go a bit. I can't control everything all of the time. Or so my mum tells me.' He tucked his phone away, then inhaled deeply. Ellie's gaze strayed to his chest again and heat rushed through her. Realising what she was doing, she looked up and found his eyes on her face.

'Let me get you a cold drink,' she said, forcing herself to turn away from him because staring at his muscles all the time was just rude. What on earth was wrong with her? She couldn't remember ever being around a man who had this effect upon her.

Jasper followed her inside, then she heard him lock the door, and it made her smile. He was so thoughtful.

'Hi Pearl,' he said. 'Something smells good in here.'

Ellie's gran pointed at her empty bowl. 'I'm trying out some of Ellie's dishes. We're extending the seasonal menu. It's an idea of Ellie's. She's ingenious and, as I always suspected, an excellent chef.'

'Gra-an!' Ellie blushed at the praise.

'Ellie has recently completed the relevant food hygiene course and other courses so she can make and prepare food here, too. I mean, she'd done the food hygiene before, but she's brushed up on everything and is all set to make some of these delicious dishes for customers, too.'

'Wow, Ellie. So it seems like you'll be staying in the village then?'

'I don't want to go back to London. I'm really enjoying being here and living with Gran again, so I think I'll hang around for a bit. Maybe even move back permanently.'

'Is that so?' He nodded thoughtfully and Ellie had to look away to buy herself a moment's grace because there was definitely something fizzing in the air between her and Jasper today. It could be her imagination because he looked so good, but it could be that their relationship was developing. The more they got to know each other, the more she liked him and the stronger the spark between them became. If it was all on her side, then she'd be very disappointed, but then why would he come here on a Sunday afternoon? He hadn't known they'd be there, but then he'd seen them and come to the door. That had to be a sign that he felt something too, surely? Ellie wished she knew for certain, wished she had the courage to ask him outright, but how could she do that? If she had imagined it all and he said he simply saw her as a friend, then she would be mortified she'd told him how she felt. Humiliation was not fun for anyone and after what had happened with Barnaby, she really didn't want to go through more. Her confidence was shaky as it was and although her gran was trying to build her up, it wouldn't take much to knock her down again. She was working at self-care and believing in herself, but it would take time and so she was too fragile to ask Jasper how he felt about her and couldn't imagine being able to do so. And this meant, of course, that she'd have to wait and see if he made a move on her. If he didn't, then she'd have her answer and if he did. *Well...*

'Have a seat, Jasper,' her gran said.

'I'm a bit … um… sweaty.' He patted his chest. 'I probably smell.'

'You smell superb, actually,' Ellie said. Jasper and her gran stared at her and she realised she'd said it out loud. 'I'll just go and get some soup and a drink for you.' She grabbed her gran's empty bowl and darted into the kitchen, her cheeks flaming and her heart racing.

What the hell, Ellie! You said that to him! He'll think you're a right weirdo now.

But he hadn't smelt unpleasant. He'd smelt clean and fresh, like the spring air and his fabric softener. He'd had a glow about him that fit people got when they exercised. In fact, he smelt so good she'd have happily wrapped her arms around him and buried her face in his chest if he'd asked her to check if she could smell sweat.

God, Ellie, are you ovulating or something?

The kitchen door opened, and her gran entered. Ellie looked away, too embarrassed to meet her gran's eyes.

'Need a hand with anything?' Her gran leant against the counter.

'No thanks. I'm fine.' Ellie hung her head as she dished out the soup, then got a glass and filled it with elderflower cordial and sparkling water. She cut some of the fresh bread and buttered it, placed it on a plate, put the soup bowl next to it and added a spoon.

'Add a little cream to the top, Ellie. It think it will work well.' Her gran got a pot of cream from the fridge, then created a swirl on the top of the soup and added a sprinkle of fresh parsley.

'Good thinking,' Ellie said.

'You OK?' her gran asked as she picked up the plate and glass.

'What? Because I just made a complete idiot of myself?' Ellie grimaced.

'Well, yes, but I don't think Jasper minded. When you came in here, he was blushing as badly as you are now. You two like each other and it's plain as day for other people to see.'

'Really?'

'Really. But you both have some baggage so just keep getting to know each other and let nature take its course.'

'Nature?' Ellie said at the door.

'Nature. Magic. Love.' Her gran shrugged. 'All of them. What's meant to be is meant to be, and I'm fairly certain that you and Jasper are meant to be.'

'That's a bit of a bold statement,' Ellie said. 'We don't even know each other very well. And we've both been hurt.'

'Well, yes, that's true on both counts, but you two can get to know each other better and … broken hearts can still heal. Trust me, Ellie, love will always find a way.'

'Any more wise words now, Gran?' Ellie laughed. 'Or should I say clichés?'

'Yes, go and feed that gorgeous man!' Her gran pushed the door open and Ellie walked through it, smiling as much inwardly as she was outwardly. She set the plate down in front of Jasper.

'This looks amazing. Thank you so much. Of course, I won't be able to run home after it, but it'll be worth it.' He flashed her a smile.

'That's OK because Ellie can walk back with you,' her gran said. 'I have to pop home now because I think I forgot to turn the iron off.' She frowned. 'Or was it my straighteners?'

'You don't use straighteners.' Ellie frowned at her gran. 'And you haven't tried the desserts I made yet.'

'That's OK, dear. Test them on Jasper and let me know what he thinks. That way we can have a genuine customer review for the notice board here and for the café Instagram. You don't mind writing a brief review, do you, Jasper?'

'Of course not.' He grinned. 'Be my pleasure.'

'Wonderful!' Ellie's gran hugged her, then squeezed Jasper's shoulder. After she'd retrieved her bag and jacket from the utility room, she smiled at them both then said, 'See you later. Have fun, you two!'

'Bye.' Ellie squinted at her gran, hoping she'd understand that she could see right through her scheming, but her gran simply waved and left the café. And Ellie wasn't at all annoyed because as much as she had wanted her gran to test out the dishes she'd made, she now had Jasper to take over that role, and it meant she had him all to herself.

What a wonderful afternoon it was turning out to be!

19

JASPER

The Easter holidays had arrived, and Jasper was taking some time off work. Two glorious weeks stretched ahead with better weather, lighter evenings and less rushing around trying to get the children to school on time. He wasn't taking the full fortnight off because his parents were having the children for a few days in the second week but this first week of the holidays was theirs.

Jasper had planned out a variety of activities for them spanning the two weeks. This morning they'd asked to go to the café and see the chickens, then to have lunch there. He'd agreed, pleased it would mean he'd get to see Ellie too.

They walked Wiggy along the beach and he splashed in the shallows with the children, then spotted a group of teenaged boys playing football. Like a shot, he was gone, racing towards the ball which he grabbed, then ran away. Jasper ran after him, and so did the teenagers, and when he caught up with Wiggy, he took the ball back, gave it to the teenagers and apologised. They were laughing though, seeing the funny side of the theft, and said Wiggy should play for the local team. After that, Jasper and the children took Wiggy home and gave him a wash, then left him snoozing in the sunlight streaming through the bifold doors.

As they walked to the garden café, Jasper savoured the salt-laced air and the warmth of the April sunshine on his skin. Mabel and Alfie chatted about school, their friends, and the holiday they were going on with their grandparents next week. When Jasper's mum had phoned and broached the subject of her and his dad having the children for a few days, Jasper's initial reaction had been panic. His mum had said they'd like to take the children to Penzance for a few days. It would only be three nights, she'd explained, but it would be nice for them and for the children. Plus, his mum had continued, it would give Jasper some time to himself. As she'd spoken, the panic had grown, threatening to engulf him.

His mum had guessed what was happening because he'd gone so quiet, and so she'd talked him through what he was feeling, helped him to address his physical reactions and then told him he had a choice about this. It didn't have to happen. He was in control. Like she'd worked magic on him just by understanding, he'd run through some relaxation techniques and soon, he felt calmer. And when he was calmer, he could accept that the children going on a holiday with their grandparents was a positive thing for them. He had agreed, and they'd worked things out in terms of dates and times, and Jasper had felt pleased with himself. Until recently, he'd have abhorred the idea of the children being anywhere other than with him, but now it was different. Now, he could see it as a reasonable request. Whether he would be able to enjoy the time when the children were away was another matter though, and so he vowed to set himself a busy schedule so he wouldn't spend the time moping and worrying.

'Nearly there, Daddy,' Alfie said as they reached the turning for the café.

Jasper smiled down at his son. 'Yes, nearly there.'

'Are you tired, Daddy?' Alfie asked.

'Not particularly. Why?'

'You are being quiet.' Alfie gave a small shrug, as if it was obvious why he'd asked.

'Oh! Sorry. I was lost in my thoughts.'

'What are you thinking about, Daddy?' Mabel tugged at his hand.

'About how happy I am that you two are going to have a holiday with your grandparents.'

'Are you sure, Daddy?' Mabel tilted her head.

'Yes. Of course, I'm sure. Why, sweetheart?'

'Well, it's a big deal for you, isn't it?'

'A big deal?' He realised he was asking a lot of questions, but he needed to understand what his children were thinking. The last thing he wanted was for them to worry about him when they should be enjoying being young.

'Yes. It will be our first holiday without you and Mummy.'

Jasper gulped. There were things going on with his children that he hadn't even registered. They could be so intuitive and so accepting, far more accepting than he often was.

'It will be a big deal for me, yes. But you'll have the best time and I can sleep later in the mornings.'

Alfie giggled. 'You never sleep late.'

'That's true, but it's because I've always got to get you two lazybones out of bed!' Jasper roared, then scooped up Alfie and threw him over one shoulder and grabbed Mabel and threw her over the other. They both squealed with delight and wriggled as they tried to get him to put them down. He kept them there until they reached the café gardens, then set them down in front of the gate.

'Daddy, that was funny!' Alfie said, his cheeks pink and his tiny teeth exposed in a wide grin.

Mabel stood with her hands on her hips, slightly out of breath, her hair coming out of her ponytail. 'That was not funny, Daddy. Look at the state of my hair now.' She reached up and tried to smooth her hair back, but it needed brushing.

'It was a bit funny.' Jasper motioned for her to turn around, then he gently removed the bobble from her hair, brushed his fingers through it and redid the style. It wasn't perfect, but it looked better than it had.

Mabel turned around and scowled at him, but then her lips twitched and she giggled. 'You bugger, Daddy!'

'Pardon?' He raised his brows, and she bit her lip.

'Oops! I mean ... you silly bear.'

'That's better. But wouldn't a bear be all growly and come grab you?' He raised his arms and growled and the children screamed and ran ahead of him. He growled again, chasing them until they'd raced around the café three times and were all puffing, laughing and red faced.

'Stop now, Daddy!' Alfie held up his hands. 'I'm so thirsty.'

'Me too. Let's get a drink.'

As they entered the café, he thought that there was nothing better than making them both laugh and seeing their small faces light up with joy. He hadn't always been good at that part of parenting. He did his best to put on a cheerful front but it could be exhausting and he knew they sometimes pretended to believe he was happy, but he caught their worried glances that told him they weren't convinced. But now, things were improving, and he intended to make them laugh as much as possible. Children should laugh and smile and run and dance and get the most out of life and it was his responsibility as their parent to ensure they had plenty of opportunities to do so.

The café was warm with spring sunshine and smelt of toasted sandwiches and coffee. His stomach grumbled, and he looked at the specials board to see what he could eat today.

The specials included Wild Garlic Soup (which he knew was delicious), Cornish crab and garden salad sandwiches, honey baked ham and cheddar toasted panini, and parmesan truffle fries in a basket. Freshly baked scones with clotted cream and strawberry jam, rhubarb tarts with Cornish custard, and lemon and elderflower drizzle cake were today's desserts. His mouth watered as he read through the delights available and he knew Ellie had something to do with the new treats on offer. Ellie had brought more to the village than her pretty smile and warmth. She'd also brought new ideas and innovation to the café her grandmother owned. And, of course, she'd brought a light into Jasper's world that he'd thought never to see again. He'd been so shut down to joy that he'd thought never to see everything positively again. However, time and then Ellie, had helped him to begin the shift from his grief-ridden impasse to a state where he felt life could be good again.

As if thinking about Ellie had summoned her, there she was, standing behind the counter. In a white and red polka dot tea dress with a wide belt and her dark hair in a high ponytail, she looked fresh and youthful. When he'd first seen her, she hadn't looked this good. Beautiful, yes, but haunted and ground down as if life had been too dark and twisted for her to thrive. But just over a month in the Cornish village had changed her physically, and he suspected, mentally, and she looked like she belonged here. Fresh air, good food, and the love of her gran had clearly had a positive effect upon Ellie, and she looked far more relaxed and definitely happier now. What had happened to her in London to make her so weighed down? He hadn't asked because he hadn't wanted to probe, but he was curious and wanted to find out. As he had discovered, it was good to talk and so it could help Ellie with her own healing if she shared things with him that she had been working through.

He turned, about to tell the children to find a seat, but they'd already gone to their favourite table and were taking their favourite books off the shelves. The café was like a home from home, and he knew how lucky they were to have this retreat to escape to when they wanted nourishment and a change of scenery. Not just that, they had the beach and the village and the coastal path and so much more on their doorstep. The enormity of it hit him then and made him wobble inwardly. All of this he had become immune to as he'd stumbled through his choking grief, but now it was right there in front of him, clear as the spring sky. Jasper had so much to live for and he was ready to embrace it all and make the most of every day.

Starting now…

'Morning!' Ellie said when he approached the counter. 'Isn't it just a beautiful day?'

'Almost as beautiful as you.' He held his breath, wondering how she'd take the compliment.

Her cheeks flushed and her eyes widened.

'Oh ... Thank you.' Her hands went to the wide belt and touched it as if to adjust it a fraction, then she slid her hands into pockets in the pretty dress.

'The colour of the dress really suits you.' *Who even are you, Jasper? Did you eat a bowl of charm for breakfast?*

The thought made him laugh, and Ellie frowned.

'What is it?' She pulled her hands from her pockets and wrapped her arms around herself.

'I wasn't laughing at you. I was laughing at myself. Rarely do I give many compliments, yet I just gave two within seconds.

'Oh.' She smiled now, but her eyes remained wary. 'OK.'

'But I meant both of them. You do look beautiful, Ellie, and that colour is perfect on you.'

'Well then, thank you.' Her shoulders dropped and he sighed with relief. He hadn't offended her, and she seemed to like the compliments. His worry had been that perhaps she would find him creepy, and he'd make her uncomfortable, but instead she appeared to be happy. 'I'm not used to being complimented,' she said, and Jasper's jaw dropped.

'What? But why?'

'My um ... My ex-boyfriend didn't compliment me much. Well, not at all. And as an actor, I was more used to being told what I wasn't and what I needed to do in order to be better. It's a harsh industry and not good for your self-esteem.'

'Well that's crazy because you should have compliments all the time and if you were my girlfriend, I'd shower you with them.'

Her eyes widened again, and Jasper froze. *What. The. Hell?* His mouth was really running away with him this morning. There must have been some honesty flakes in with the bowl of charm.

'I mean...' He sighed. 'Sorry, Ellie, it's been a busy morning. Wiggy ran off on the beach and stole a ball and we had to chase him all the way along the sand until I could grab him. The group of teenagers were pretty good about it but then we walked here and perhaps I've just had too much sun. Not that I didn't mean what I said to you because I absolutely do, but I know I'm also being rather chatty.' He laughed and rubbed a hand over the back of his neck. 'Sorry.'

'You have nothing to apologise for, Jasper. Nothing at all.'

They stood holding each other's gaze until Jasper felt a tugging at his T-shirt. He turned to find Alfie hopping from one leg to the other. 'I need a wee wee,' he said.

'OK, go on then. You know where the toilets are.'

'I just wanted to let you know, so you didn't think I was lost.' Alfie grinned at him.

'Thank you.' Jasper ruffled his son's hair. He would go with Alfie if they were anywhere else, but the toilets were just through the door at the rear of the café and there was no other way in there. Normally, Alfie insisted on going in alone at the café, as he liked to feel like a big boy, just like he was in school.

'I guess I should order some drinks,' Jasper said. 'What's good today?'

'We have a peach iced tea that's very refreshing.' Ellie smiled.

'I'll take three of those please and after I've checked with the children, I'll order some lunch.'

'No problem. Go on over and I'll bring the drinks to you.' He was about to turn away when Ellie said, 'Oh, and Jasper?'

'Yes?'

'You look really good today, too. That blue suits you.'

Jasper ran a hand over his beard and smiled shyly. 'That's very kind of you.' When he'd dressed that morning, he'd thought the blue of the T-shirt brought out the blue of his eyes and he'd wondered if Ellie would notice. Him! Caring about what a woman thought about him.

But as he walked over to the corner table, it hit him it wasn't just any woman he was thinking about. It was Ellie, and she was someone very special indeed. It had even crossed his mind that Kimberley would have liked her if they had met.

20

ELLIE

The first week of the school Easter holidays had been very enjoyable for Ellie. She'd worked at the café alongside her gran, served some of her new dishes and looked forward to Jasper's daily visits with the children. Just waking up each day and knowing that she'd see his handsome face, hear his deep voice and spend time near him and his children made her spring out of bed in the morning. A voice at the back of her mind had warned her more than once that this was madness and that she barely knew the man, he was a single parent with lots of responsibilities and that he couldn't possibly be interested in her, but it was like she couldn't help herself. Leaving London and living near the sea again, along with all the laughing she did with her gran, the home-cooked meals and escaping the pressure that she'd been under for years had changed her. She felt like a butterfly emerging from its silken prison; the feeling of stretching her wings without fear of judgment was exquisite and liberating. When she'd lived in London, she'd felt insignificant, unworthy, and unlovable. Back in Cornwall she felt safe, loved, and that she was, quite simply, enough.

She'd finished early this afternoon because the café had fallen quiet and her gran had told her to take a breather. Ellie had tried to resist, telling her gran that she'd stay and help, but her gran had a friend coming in for a drink and a chat anyway, plus Thora was working too, so Ellie was free to please herself.

She left the café and walked along the road that led down to the village in one direction and to the beach in the other. The cliffs stretched out into the sea, craggy and grey, weather-worn and patchy with greenery. A natural inlet that provided protection from the worst of the weather led to the small, pretty harbour.

The tide was out, and the sand on the beach gleamed in the spring sunshine, freckled with shells, pebbles and seaweed. A few families sat on towels or deckchairs, watching as children played in the sand or raced around the beach. In the water, she could see several swimmers and kayaks and further out, small boats bobbed on the horizon. Seagulls squawked as they soared high above the beach, their feathers white against the blue of the sky, and a few jostled for space on top of a bin on the path that led down to the sand.

Spotting a brown dog chasing a ball at the far end of the beach, she paused and watched. Was that Wiggy? It looked like it could be. Her stomach fluttered with a thrilling mix of excitement and nerves, as if butterflies were dancing inside her. She gently patted her stomach, feeling the soft warmth radiating through her fingertips, a comforting gesture to calm her racing thoughts. The anticipation of seeing Jasper hung in the air like a tangible presence, but she cautiously reminded herself not to let her hopes soar too high. This was foolish behaviour, and she should know better.

When she reached the path that overlooked the sand, she paused and gazed across the beach again. The dog was running in and out of the sea now and a tall figure stood watching while two smaller ones played with the dog. It must be Jasper and the children. She would take a closer took. It would be nice to see him away from the café.

Her hands went to her hair and tucked the strands that had escaped her ponytail behind her ears, then she slipped off her trainers and socks, tucked the socks into her trainers, picked them up and padded across the sand.

The closer she got to the sea, the more powerful the salt-laced breeze became. It toyed with her hair, making the loose tendrils tickle her skin, and flapped her cardigan open across her chest. She breathed deeply, savoured the warmth of the spring sunshine on her skin and the sensation of the cool, damp sand beneath her soles. Surely there was nothing better than walking along the sand and breathing in the sea air? The sense of freedom it offered was incredible, and she was grateful to be there, grateful for the sensations, grateful to be able to call this beautiful location home.

The dog came racing out of the sea and bounded up the beach. The man turned and she saw she'd been right, it was Jasper, then she heard him shouting at the dog. His voice carried on the breeze, but the dog kept running. Running. Running. Jasper turned back to the children and said something and she saw them hold hands then he ran after Wiggy, hands around his mouth as he shouted. But Wiggy had set his sights on something and there was evidently no changing his mind.

And as he got closer, Ellie realised what it was.

Wiggy was running straight towards her, his mouth open and tongue lolling, his strides large. Water dropped from his fur and sand flew into the air as he ran, a large brown soaking-wet dog.

Ellie looked around but there was nowhere to go, so she held up her hands and turned slightly to the side, but Wiggy collided with her and knocked her off balance. She spun and flung out her arms, but it was too late and she went up in the air and then down again. She hit the sand with a thump, knocking the breath from her and causing stars to spin before her eyes.

'Ellie!' Jasper's voice.

Cold hands on her face. Her shoulders through the thin cardigan as he helped her to sit. Touching her face again. Large hands that checked her over as Jasper asked if she was OK, if she was hurt, if he could do anything. Then his slightly shaky voice reprimanding the dog for knocking her over before he crouched next to Ellie and peered into her eyes.

'Ellie, I'm so sorry. Wiggy didn't mean to do that. He must have recognised you from the shoreline and he ran off so quickly, before I realised what was happening. He's never done that before. I'm so embarrassed. Are you hurt?'

He cupped her chin and gently moved her head from side to side.

'Ellie?' Concern in his beautiful eyes making them cloudy as a stormy sky.

'I'm OK,' she said, catching her breath. 'Just a bit winded.'

'I'm so sorry. I saw him knock you over and couldn't get here quickly enough.'

Ellie glanced over at the dog. Wiggy stood there grinning at her like he was her best friend in the world, his tail wagging so hard his whole bottom was wiggling.

'I guess he was excited to see me.' Ellie shifted on the sand and winced.

'You are hurt!' Jasper slid the end of Wiggy's lead over his hand and took her shoulders with both hands. His eyes scanned her face. He was so close she could smell the salt on his skin along with hints of cedarwood and bergamot. It was fresh and yet earthy at the same time, and inwardly she swooned, yearning to press her face against his skin to see if he smelt even better up close.

'No, I'm fine.' She moved to her knees and then to her feet, but as her left foot connected with the sand, a pain shot through her ankle and she stumbled. But Jasper was there, and before she could try to put her foot down again, he scooped her up in his arms in one fluid movement, pressing her against his rock-hard chest.

Blinking up at him, she said, 'Jasper, you'd better put me down or you'll injure yourself.'

His laughter rumbled through his chest, sending tingles reverberating to her core. The heat of a desire she'd never experienced before washed over her and she struggled to breathe. Warmth filled her cheeks, and she tried to move in his arms, but he had her pinned against him, so all she could do was place her right hand on his chest as if to push away from him. Instead, her hand betrayed her, resting on his pectoral muscle, and the heat in her cheeks roared to flames.

'You're light as a feather, Ellie. Don't worry about me.'

This man was big and strong, and Ellie felt more feminine than she'd ever imagined feeling. As he cradled her with ease, a mixture of awe and fragility washed over Ellie. The physical disparity between their heights made her feel small and delicate in comparison. She could sense her muscles relaxing, surrendering to his strength, as if her body instinctively trusted him to protect and support her.

'Here they come,' he said, and she followed his gaze to see Mabel and Alfie running towards them.

'Daddy!' Mabel called. 'Is Ellie OK?'

'Why don't you ask her?' he said.

'Ellie?' Mabel's face contorted. 'Are you all right?'

Jasper shifted her in his arms so he could crouch down and Ellie found herself perched on his knee, one muscular arm supporting her while the other steadied Wiggy.

'I'm fine.' Ellie nodded.

'Are you sure?' Mabel came closer, one small hand outstretched like she was approaching an anxious animal. She laid the hand on Ellie's arm and then moved it to her cheek. 'We thought you were hurt.'

'Mabel said you were dead,' Alfie said with a one shoulder shrug. 'I said you weren't, but she was crying.'

'Was not!' Mabel nudged her brother.

'Was so!' Alfie nudged Mabel back.

'No, I'm not … d—hurt.' Ellie shook her head. She peered up at Jasper from underneath her lashes and saw that he was watching his children closely. The poor things had thought she was hurt, and she knew why this would be an issue for them.

'Thank goodness.' Mabel flung her arms around Ellie's neck and hugged her. Ellie froze for a moment, then she wrapped her arms around the little girl. Not to be outdone, Alfie wriggled between Ellie and his dad and hugged her, too. Ellie hugged them back, conscious of the fact that she was still on Jasper's knee and that his one arm was still around her back while his two children embraced her. And it didn't feel weird. This little family had lost so much and yet they were caring and affectionate, and they seemed to care about her too.

'Come on then, kids, we should head home,' Jasper said softly. 'I think Ellie needs to come with us and have some ice on her ankle.'

'And ice cream!' Alfie grinned as he stepped away from the hug. 'It will make you feel much better, Ellie.'

'I'm sure it will.' She smiled at him, then looked down at Mabel who was still hugging her. 'You OK, poppet?' she asked, stroking Mabel's hair.

Mabel nodded, then let go of Ellie and stepped back. 'I was worried about you.'

'I'm all right. I promise. Apart from having a wet bottom.'

Alfie giggled, and Mabel smiled. 'Is it really wet?'

'Yes.'

'I can vouch for that,' Jasper said. 'With it being on my leg.'

'I'm so sorry!' Ellie made to stand up, but he shook his head.

'Hold on, Missy.' He helped her to stand on her good foot while he supported her, then he crouched in front of her. 'Climb on.'

'What?'

'Get on my back and I'll carry you.'

'You can't give me a piggyback all the way to your house.'

'He's very strong, Ellie,' Mabel said. 'He can carry you and run at the same time.'

'God, no!' Ellie's hand flew to her chest.

'I won't run, but I will carry you,' Jasper said over his shoulder. 'Come on!'

Ellie looked from Jasper to Mabel to Alfie and then to Wiggy, who was still attached to his owner by his lead, and even his eyes seemed to tell her to hurry.

'OK then.' She slid her arms around Jasper's neck, then her legs around his waist and he got to his feet, tucking one hand underneath her bottom to hoist her up. When he had her settled in a comfortable position, he secured Wiggy's lead to his belt, then he was able to hold her thighs with his hands to make sure she didn't slip.

'Comfy?' he asked.

Pressed against his back with her arms around his neck and her legs around his waist, Ellie fought the urge to make an inappropriate joke. His children were there, after all, and they were in a public place. There was nothing intimate about this at all, just one friend carrying another because she'd hurt her ankle.

'Yes.' Her voice squeaked out and so she cleared her throat then tried again. 'I'm good thanks.'

Good! That was the understatement of the year!

'Come on then. Let's get home.'

Jasper strode up the beach along with Mabel and Alfie on either side of him and Wiggy trotting along a few steps in front. Ellie wondered what people would think if they saw them like this and decided she really didn't care if it looked strange. She might have been knocked over by a dog, but she'd been tended to and cuddled, and now she was being carried to a place where she would be given ice cream. It wasn't her worst day by far. In fact, it was turning out to be one of her best days ever…

21
ELLIE

When they reached his home, Jasper opened the door and they all went inside. He carried Ellie through to the lounge and set her down carefully on the sofa.

'Mabel, take Alfie up to wash his hands and put some clean clothes on and I'll sort the ice cream.'

'Yes, Daddy!'

The children left the lounge and Jasper crouched down next to Ellie. 'I'll get you some dry clothes and show you where you can change.'

'Thank you.' Ellie shuffled to the edge of the sofa. 'My jeans are almost dry, I think, but I don't want to get your lovely sofa sandy.' She looked down at the cream sofa with its plump cushions. It must have cost a bit, and she didn't want to ruin it.

'Don't worry. It's easy to clean. When Kimberley said she wanted a cream sofa, I told her she was mad. With two children, cream is not exactly a practical colour, but she had her heart set on it so we agreed on a wipe clean material.' His expression changed and a small line appeared between his brows. 'She always got what she wanted.' He gave a small laugh, then shook his head.

'It was a good choice. It's very nice.' Ellie smoothed a hand over a cushion.

'Kimberley liked quality things.' He went to the door. 'Back in a bit.'

He left the room with Wiggy hot on his heels. Ellie took the opportunity to look around. The lounge was bright and airy: white walls, white blinds on the two large windows and the cream L-shaped sofa. The floors were hardwood, and there was a reclaimed wood mantelpiece above the large log burner set into the chimney space. Framed photographs sat on the mantelpiece and, above it hung a wooden heart decorated with dried lavender. Overwhelmed by curiosity about the photographs, Ellie got to her feet and hobbled over to look.

Baby pictures of Mabel and Alfie, some of them together, and one of Jasper and the children playing in the café's summer gardens were displayed, their vibrant colours and happy expressions hinting at warm summer days. In the background of one she could see the café and just make out her gran in the window. A wedding photograph sat in the middle of the mantel, and it made her heart squeeze. There was Jasper, tall and handsome, if perhaps not as filled out as he was now. His beard was closely cropped, his hair longer and wavy, and he was clearly younger. He looked like he could have been a Viking surfer, tall, tanned and healthy. His gaze was locked on the beautiful woman beside him, as if he was oblivious to everything and everyone else. Wearing a simple white dress and a pearl band in her dark hair, Kimberley didn't need any other adornments because she glowed with beauty and joy. She was gazing at the camera, laughing, and Jasper's arm was around her waist, his hand resting on her hip. They were young and filled with hope and Ellie felt very sad for them in that moment. Jasper had lost so much and then had to keep going for his children. What an amazing man he was, strong not just in body but mentally and emotionally too. In that moment, her feelings for him deepened.

'Ellie.'

She started at his voice and turned to face him, worried he'd be annoyed that she'd been snooping, but there was no judgement in his eyes.

'I'm so sorry, Jasper, for your loss. Kimberley was beautiful.'

She saw him inhale deeply, his Adam's apple bobbing visibly as he gulped.

'Thank you.' He held up some clothing as he approached her. 'Let me help you to the downstairs toilet so you can change.'

When he left her, she closed the door and set the clothes on a shelf behind the toilet, then she removed her cardigan and vest top before sliding down her jeans. She tried not to overthink the fact that she was in a man's house in her underwear and focused on folding her clothes, then dressing in the items Jasper had brought for her. She pulled the pale blue T-shirt over her head and slid her arms through the sleeves. It was a man's size and it drowned her, but it was soft and smelt of Jasper's fabric softener. Reaching for the other garment, she found a pair of jogging bottoms that she put on by sitting on the toilet lid and sliding one leg through at a time then shuffling from side to side so she could pull them up. They were baggy too, but also soft and warm. She tied the cord at the waist, rolled up the legs a few times then stood up and picked up her clothes.

Catching sight of her reflection in the mirror above the sink, she winced. Her ponytail had slid down her head and the soft curls at her temple had burst out like springs, affected by the breeze and the water when she'd fallen. She pulled the band from her hair and shook it out, then combed it through with her fingers. It wasn't perfect, but it would have to do. Besides, she had some colour in her cheeks and a light in her eyes that made them appear to sparkle from within. She smiled at herself and then laughed because she was standing in a friend's downstairs toilet wearing his clothes and nursing a sore ankle because his over excitable dog had knocked her off her feet. You couldn't write it…

OK then, it was time for ice cream.

22
JASPER

When Ellie walked into his kitchen wearing his jogging bottoms and T-shirt, Jasper's heart jumped, then pounded like a drum in his chest. His clothes were huge on her, hiding her soft feminine curves and drawing his attention to her beautiful face and those striking green eyes the colour of summer fields. Her black hair tumbled over her shoulders and tiny curls caressed her hairline. Catching his eyes on her, she blushed in the way he found adorable and he smiled as warmth filled his chest.

'Thanks for these.' She gestured at herself and he noticed that she'd rolled the legs of the jogging bottoms up a few times.

'Sorry they're so big.'

'If they weren't, you'd look strange wearing them.' She smiled as she hobbled over to the island.

'Here, sit down.' He pulled out a stool and helped her to sit on it, keeping the weight off her sore ankle.

'Thanks.'

'I'll sort some ice for that ankle and then we can have a think about what you want to eat.'

'I thought we were having ice cream?' She raised her raven black brows.

'We are, but I also thought you might want something more substantial.'

'I don't want you to go to any trouble,' she said.

'It's no trouble, and I have to cook for the children, so I figured we'd just as well eat, too. If that's what you want.' He paused. 'If you'd prefer to go straight home, I can drop you in the car though?'

She glanced over at the bifold doors and then back at him. 'What would you like me to do?' she asked. 'I'm sorry, but I'm not very good at this. You've already done a lot for me and I don't want to overstay my welcome. I hate getting on people's nerves.'

'What?' He frowned. Where had this come from? 'Why would you think that?'

She went to stand, so he hurried to her side and took her arm.

'Don't put that foot down yet,' he said softly. 'But please tell me why you'd think I want you to go.'

'I ... I don't like to annoy people.'

'How could you annoy anyone?' Before he could stop himself, he'd reached out and brushed her hair behind her ear, stroked the soft skin of her cheek. Her pupils dilated and her lips parted, and she held his gaze. 'I don't see how anyone could find you anything other than enchanting.'

'Y-you find me enchanting?'

He nodded. His voice was trapped in his throat. A surge of warmth spread through his chest, a tingling sensation that awakened dormant emotions. It felt as if a fire within him had been rekindled. Ellie's presence was like a gentle breeze, stirring the layers of his being, breathing life into his weary bones. Ellie was bringing him back — back to himself, back to life, back to being a man.

'You are utterly enchanting.' His voice was gruff with emotion, with desire.

She blinked at him and inhaled shakily. 'So are you.'

He slid his hand over her shoulder and entwined his fingers in the hair at her nape while he placed the other hand on her chest so his fingers splayed over her collarbones. His hand rose and fell with every breath she took, and he could feel her heart racing. She was warm and soft and she smelt incredible, like amber and vanilla, saltwater and coconut. He moved closer so he could bury his face in her hair and she turned in his arms so she was against his chest, her arms around his waist.

They stayed that way for a while, their hearts beating together, their breathing in sync, and Jasper felt something happening to him. For so long, he'd had a tight knot in his shoulders that had created a pain so sharp it sometimes took his breath away. He was conscious every day of holding himself rigid so he'd stay strong, of being solid in case he weakened and crumbled, but it came with consequences including tension and aches. Sometimes it spread up to his jaw and his forehead and gave him headaches, as well as making him grind his teeth at night. It wasn't healthy, and he knew it, but he was afraid of losing control, of weakening and not being strong enough for his children. And with this came loneliness. He was so incredibly lonely. It had been years since he'd held a woman in his arms and now, Ellie was soothing him, easing the tension from his muscles and his heart, relaxing him so he could let go of the pain. His vision blurred and he swallowed as emotion surged inside him. There was so much to release and now he had begun, he wouldn't be able to stop. He didn't want to stop.

When he pulled back slightly, he moved his hand and brushed his thumb over her full lips, touched them the way he imagined kissing them. Ellie gasped and peered up at him. Her eyes flashed, and his body responded in a way he'd forgotten it could.

'Ellie, I—'

'NO! Alfie, that's not yours to show!'

Jasper jumped back, and Ellie wobbled on the stool. He held out his hands to steady her, then tucked them in his pockets as Mabel and Alfie entered the kitchen. They were squabbling as they tried to hold something up to show Ellie.

'Daddy, tell Alfie!' Mabel's small face was bright pink as she tried to pull the book from Alfie while Alfie was close to tears.

'I want to show her,' Alfie whined.

'What is it?' Jasper went to his children and eased their hands apart. His breath caught in his throat. It was a small photograph album that Kimberley had made after having each child. It went up to three years ago, the last photo printed just a week before her death. Jasper found it hard to look at, but the children loved it and he understood how important it was to them.

'I want to show Ellie,' Alfie said, his eyes shining.

'I'd love to see it,' Ellie said, gingerly getting down from the stool.

'Tell you what. Let's get you back to the lounge and the children can sit on the sofa with you. The three of you can look at it together while I make dinner,' he said.

'Sounds good to me.' Ellie accepted his arm, and they went to the lounge. Once she was settled on the sofa with Mabel and Alfie on either side of her, Jasper went to the kitchen and got the bag of ice chips and a towel. He took them to the lounge and helped Ellie to raise her leg onto a cushion on the coffee table.

'OK if I roll this up a bit more?' He pointed at the leg of the jogging bottoms.

'Of course.' Ellie smiled.

He gently rolled it up to her calf, then covered her ankle with the towel and placed the bag of ice on top. 'How's that?'

'Brilliant.'

'Good. Right then … What do we fancy for dinner?' His heart was still pounding and his throat was tight but he felt alive. He wasn't sure if the children's interruption had been a good thing or not, but at some point, he would have the chance to be alone with Ellie and then they could continue where they had left off.

'Ice cream!' Alfie shouted.

'I think we should have something before ice cream.'

'Pizza!' Mabel said. 'Can we have your homemade pizza, Daddy, with lots of cheese and tomatoes and peppers and shrooms.'

'Shrooms?' Ellie asked.

'Mush-rooms!' Mabel giggled. 'Daddy calls them shrooms.'

'I can make pizza. That OK with you, Ellie? No allergies or anything you really dislike?'

'Nothing at all. Except for liver and, well, all offal.' Ellie pulled a face, and Mabel and Alfie giggled.

'What's offal?' Mabel asked. Ellie explained, then Mabel made a vomiting noise. 'That's disgusting!'

'I would eat it,' Alfie said, puffing out his chest to show how brave he was.

'You would not. You won't even eat sprouts and they're a vegetable and not an animal's insides.' Mabel sniggered, and Alfie scowled at her before shaking his head.

'You're right, Mabel, I wouldn't eat that. And sprouts are yucky!'

Jasper met Ellie's eyes and grinned. She was clearly finding this conversation amusing.

'I'll make liver-free pizza then.'

'And we can look at the baby photos and ones of our mummy,' Mabel said, snuggling closer to Ellie.

Jasper left them to it and went to the kitchen, hoping he had enough mozzarella in the fridge to make some tasty pizzas. He realised he hadn't checked if Ellie liked thick or thin base pizza, so he went back to the lounge to ask, but he froze in the doorway, unable to disturb the scene before him. Ellie sat sandwiched between his children, holding the photograph album while Mabel turned the pages. Alfie had his one small arm wrapped around Ellie's shoulders and he was resting his head on her. His other hand was toying with her long hair, twirling it around his fingers the way he did with his taggy blanket. Mabel's face was animated as she described each photo to Ellie and Ellie listened intently, asking questions. Mabel paused every so often to smile up at Ellie. It was an idyllic scene of contentment that made Jasper realise it wasn't just him who'd been missing an adult female presence. His children had bonded with Ellie as if they had known her forever, and he believed this was due to Ellie's kindness and warmth. She had a good heart, and they were all comfortable with her. It was wonderful and yet scary because if something were to happen, then Jasper and his children would need to cope with losing Ellie. Whether she left the village or became involved with someone else or … Or something worse still.

He shuddered, then gave himself a firm inward shake. Right now, Ellie was there with them and they were all enjoying her company. Nothing came with guarantees, and he had to let go of his need to control everything. Some things were beyond his control. Some things were beyond human comprehension and would simply be the way they were.

For now, he would push his concerns to one side and focus on the here and now. He hadn't always done that enough and so it was something he wanted to practise more going forwards.

Back in the kitchen, he went about making the best pizzas Ellie had ever tasted. He'd make thick and thin crust pizzas just to cover all bases. As he began kneading the dough, a warm sense of contentment spread throughout his body. The comforting murmur of voices floating from the lounge soothed him, easing the tension in his shoulders. The weight of responsibility seemed to momentarily lift as he realised he had someone else to rely on, a temporary respite from the constant demands of being a single parent.

23

ELLIE

As Mabel and Alfie talked through the photographs in the album, Ellie's chest ached for them. The photographs were beautiful portrayals of a young family with so much to be happy about and so much ahead of them. Even the early photographs of the first few days and weeks after the birth of each baby, when Kimberley and Jasper were sleep deprived and adjusting to parenthood, were lovely. And the love between Jasper and his wife was clear in every photograph. They'd had a special bond, the kind that Ellie had hoped to have with Barnaby but found lacking. It was the love that she suspected only came to the lucky ones and that she had grown to accept would never happen for her. But perhaps not everyone needed to have that all-consuming devotion and intense attraction to someone. Perhaps some people just found someone who was kind to them and who they found attractive enough to enjoy spending time with. And yet, the more time she spent with Jasper, the more she liked him and the more attractive she found him. Earlier in the kitchen, when he'd touched her, she'd felt things she'd never experienced before. Her heart had raced, and her core had longed for more. She had yearned for him to kiss her, hold her, and lift her into those big, powerful arms. For him to press his body against hers and to touch her as only a lover would. Was it possible that Jasper could be the love she'd never had before? Her heart sank a fraction. Jasper had loved and lost. Could he love again or would any future partner always live in Kimberley's shadow?

She looked at the children on either side of her. Jasper and Kimberley's love had created these two mini human beings, and they were perfect. Absolutely perfect. But whatever he might still feel for his wife, she was gone and nothing could change that. He deserved happiness and to love again, and she felt sure Kimberley, the woman in the photographs who looked at Jasper with so much love in her eyes, would want her husband to be happy again. She would want him to love and be loved just as she'd want her children to be loved. What was it they said? It takes a village to raise a child? You could never have too many people to love a child, and she already cared about Mabel and Alfie. She also cared about Jasper. Could that be enough? Could there be something other than friendship in their future?

When Jasper returned to the lounge bringing with him the delicious aromas of toasted cheese and garlic, she wondered how the scene looked to him. Did seeing his children with Ellie make him happy or scared? He had already lost one partner, so would he be able to risk his heart by loving another? Nothing in life came with guarantees, and no one lived forever. Was Jasper strong enough and brave enough to risk his heart again?

Was Ellie?

'Right then, who's hungry?' Jasper asked.

'Me!' the children chorused.

'Go and wash your hands and then we can eat.'

'Yes, Daddy.' Mabel put the photograph album on the table, then waited for Alfie to follow her.

'Shall we eat in here?' Jasper looked at the coffee table. 'We don't usually, but it might be nice for today.'

Ellie shifted her position on the sofa and moved her leg from the cushion on the coffee table. 'I don't mind.'

'How's the ankle?' Jasper watched her move her foot.

'A lot better, actually. I don't think it's even a bad sprain. The ice has helped.'

'That's brilliant, but take it easy for a few days because you don't want to put too much pressure on it.'

'I will.'

'OK … I'll get everything sorted and bring it through.' He rubbed a hand over his head. 'Ellie … um… sorry for earlier in the kitchen. That wasn't like me. I don't … I haven't … been with anyone … not since Kimberley.' He was looking anywhere but at her as he said the words, and she could see how hard this was for him. 'I guess what I'm trying to say is that I don't make a habit of this. Women don't come to my home or spend time with my children and I don't … hug women either.'

Now he met her gaze, and she nodded. 'I know that, Jasper. I didn't think you did.'

'Good. But …' He sighed and shook his head. 'With you … God, this is hard to say because I'm so out of practice but… I really like you, Ellie.'

'I like you too. Thank you for bringing me to your home and trusting me with your children. It means a lot.'

'Thank you for coming and for being so good with Mabel and Alfie. They clearly like you and trust you. Showing you the photographs like that, it's just…' He fell silent, a muscle in his jaw twitching, his blue eyes glistening.

'I know.' She smiled, emotion making her own throat ache.

'I'll um … get the food.' He pointed a thumb over his shoulder.

'Can I help?'

'Stay there and rest that ankle. But when the children come back, can you check that Alfie actually used soap and didn't just dip his fingertips into the water?'

'Of course I will.' Ellie laughed.

'Thanks.' Jasper returned to the kitchen and Ellie sat back on the sofa. In just weeks, her life had changed dramatically, but she had no regrets. The life she'd thought she wanted hadn't made her happy, and she much preferred the version she was living now.

24
PEARL

Standing in the spring sunshine, Pearl smiled as she watched the village children racing around the gardens. There were shouts of excitement and lots of laughter as they located Easter eggs and added them to their baskets. It was a tradition to hold the village Easter Egg Hunt at the café gardens and every year, Pearl hoped the weather would be nice. It wasn't quite the same watching the poor children wearing raincoats and wellies as they squelched around in search of eggs that would surely be wet by the time they found them. But today was glorious: bright blue sky, warm sunshine and a balmy sea breeze.

She looked around for Ellie, then spotted her with Jasper's children. Alfie was glued to her side while Mabel walked on ahead, turning every so often to give her younger brother instructions. Ellie had helped Pearl to set up the clues earlier that morning and to hide the eggs, but she appeared to be feigning ignorance as to their whereabouts so the children to work things out for themselves.

What pleased Pearl was how contented Ellie looked with the children. She'd never thought of her granddaughter as being someone keen to have children of her own, but she was a natural with Mabel and Alfie. She knew how to speak to them, how to reassure them, and they responded to her happily and confidently. Three days ago, Ellie had spent the afternoon and evening with Jasper and the children. When Ellie had returned home, she'd been glowing with happiness. Apparently, she'd sprained her ankle at the beach and Jasper had taken her home to put ice on it, but then invited her to stay for food. Looking at them now, she thought, an outsider who didn't know them might think they were a family.

She patted a finger on her lips as she thought about that. Mabel and Alfie had lost their mum when they were very young. Jasper was an amazing dad to them and he had other female role models around for them, but it would never replace having a mum. Kimberley had been a lovely person, but she was no longer here. Pearl knew well that you didn't need to be someone's biological mother to love them and raise them. Wouldn't it be wonderful if Jasper found love again, a love that brought joy to him and his children, filling their home with laughter and warmth?

'You look deep in thought.'

Pearl turned to Jasper, who'd just emerged from the café, a tray of drinks in his hands.

'Always.' She laughed.

'Ellie is amazing with the children,' he said, gazing over at them.

'I know. She's a natural.' Pearl nodded, then she turned her gaze back to Jasper. 'And what about you and Ellie?'

He lifted his chin, and his eyes widened slightly.

'It's all right, Jasper. You can be honest with me.'

He blew out a breath. 'I, um … I don't really know how to answer that question, Pearl.'

'Truthfully, sweetheart.'

'OK … um…' He looked down at the tray and shifted it around in his hands. 'Ellie is … a very special person and I enjoy spending time with her.'

'I'm glad.' Pearl placed a hand on his arm. 'Happiness isn't guaranteed in this life, so … as I've said before … when you find it, grab it.'

'Yeah … It's not the easy though, right?' He looked up and she could see that his blue eyes were cloudy. 'I have to put the children first and to ensure that all my decisions are the right ones for them.'

'This is true. But doesn't their dad being happy have a knock-on effect for them too? And surely the one thing we should teach our children is that they have a right to be happy and a right to be loved.'

Jasper smiled. 'My mum said something similar to me recently.'

'Now… I know I'm biased because Ellie is my blood, but she really is a special soul and she would be good for all of you. She hasn't had an easy time of things over the years and I know she's still working out what she wants from life too, but she also has a lot of love to give to the right person.'

'I get what you're saying.' Jasper's eyes roamed in Ellie's direction again, and Pearl watched as his expression softened. There was definitely something there, and Pearl hoped

Jasper would make peace with his feelings for Ellie and his desire to protect the children. It was possible for him to have the happiness she felt certain Ellie could bring to his life, just as Ellie could find hers with him.

'Fluidity, Jasper, is a marvellous thing. Move with your feelings. Know that it is OK not to be fully in control at all times. You are a father, but you are also a man and you are permitted to want things for yourself.'

'Thanks, Pearl.' He leant forwards and kissed her cheek, holding the tray carefully so as not to spill the drinks.

'Now have fun darling. It's a beautiful day for it.'

Jasper crossed the grass to Ellie and his children and Pearl smiled at the way Ellie's face lit up when Jasper reached her. Call her a romantic old fool, but she had a feeling they could well be falling in love.

25

ELLIE

A few days had passed since the Easter Egg Hunt at the café. Ellie had thoroughly enjoyed the day, especially the picnic afterwards that she'd shared on the grass with Jasper, Mabel, and Alfie. They'd eaten tiny cheese and leek pasties, salmon and cucumber sandwiches, zesty lemon tarts, and plenty of chocolate. Alfie had been keen to share his eggs with Ellie and she'd become choked up when he'd climbed onto her lap after he'd eaten and snuggled into her. He was a sweet child, and he seemed to be as fond of her as she was of him. She also adored Mabel, who chatted to her easily now and seemed to have thousands of questions about everything. Mabel had then suggested that they do one more sweep of the gardens in case anyone had missed any eggs. Ellie had looked down at Alfie to ask if he wanted to go too and discovered that he had nodded off in her lap. Jasper had got up and told Mabel he would take her around the gardens and Mabel had taken his hand. As they'd walked away, Ellie had glanced over at the café to see her gran watching her from the doorway, beaming. She had given Ellie a thumbs up and Ellie had returned it. Cuddling Alfie was wonderful, and she wanted to be there for him more and more, the same with Jasper and Mabel too.

She was on her way to Jasper's house now because Mabel and Alfie were going away with his parents for a few days. He'd looked anxious when he'd told her about it, so she wanted to cheer him up if she could. She'd packed a basket with some of the Easter foods she'd prepared for the café so she could make Jasper lunch. It was the least she could do after the meals he'd made for her recently and after how well he'd taken care of her after she'd hurt her ankle. Said ankle was fine now, and she was certain it was because Jasper had acted so quickly when she'd first been injured.

When she reached Jasper's home, she rang the bell and waited, conscious that she was on the doorbell camera.

'Hello there!' he said as he opened the door, looking so handsome he took her breath away. In a fitted charcoal T-shirt and black cargo shorts, he looked muscular and toned. His stomach was washboard flat and his upper arms stretched the sleeves. His military-style haircut was fresh, and his golden beard and the golden hairs on his muscular forearms shone in the sunlight.

'Hi.' She felt suddenly shy as he invited her inside. After all, when she'd been here before, so had the children, but now it was just the two of them. 'How are you doing?'

He led the way through to the kitchen. 'Not too bad, actually. It wasn't easy seeing them off this morning, but they'll be with my parents and have a great time, I'm sure of it.'

'I brought lunch.' She held up the basket. 'It's nothing fancy, just some bits from the café.'

'That's really kind of you.' He accepted the basket and set it on the island. 'Would you like a drink? Tea? Coffee?'

'Something cold would be great, thanks.' She sat on a stool at the island and a flashback hit her. Jasper had held her, laced his fingers through her hair, and almost kissed her before they'd been interrupted.

'How about some wine?' he asked. 'I rarely keep much alcohol here but I thought that seeing as how I have a few days without the children, I could relax a bit.' He showed her a bottle of white straight from the fridge, and she nodded.

'Wine would be great. I have the rest of the day off.'

'Excellent!'

He opened the wine and got two glasses from the cupboard. After he'd filled them, he handed her one.

'Here's to relaxing.' He frowned. 'And maybe catching up on some sleep.'

'Cheers.' They clinked glasses, then Ellie sipped the wine. It had a floral aroma and tasted of apricots. It was refreshing and delicious. She took another sip, then set her glass on the island. 'So what have you got planned for the next few days?'

'I have some work to finish, and I thought I'd try to empty the washing basket. It's a never-ending task with the children filling it constantly.'

'Gran used to say the same about me and I was just one person.' Ellie laughed.

'Tell me about it. And Wiggy makes his own washing piles for me.'

The dog wagged his tail from his bed near the bifold doors, then stretched out and closed his eyes again.

'Will he be OK with the children gone?' Ellie asked.

'Yeah … He's used to them going off to school in the mornings, so he probably won't notice until later and I'll keep him busy, anyway.' Jasper sipped his wine. 'This is tasty.'

'It's lovely.'

They fell quiet and Ellie looked from her glass to the dog and out of the bifold doors. 'You really do have the most beautiful view here.'

'It's not bad, is it?'

Ellie got up and went to the doors and gazed out at the sea. Her vision blurred as memories washed over her. She had loved living in the village growing up and had many happy memories there, but there were also sad ones. Her grampa had lost his life in that water, had sacrificed himself for another. But she had also swum there herself, spent happy days at the beach and walking the coastal path. Any location would hold a plethora of memories and emotions, both good and bad, happy and sad. Surely that was the way and wherever you went in life, it would always be the same. No one could outrun their past. Life was hard, but it was also incredibly beautiful; it brought so much joy while it also brought pain. Jasper had been happy here but also lost his wife. Her gran loved the location, but had lost her husband to the sea. Her parents had been happy together for a while but had then parted ways and left a long time ago. People would come and people would go, whether by choice or as their lives came to an end, but the sea, the sky, the sand, the cliffs, and the village would continue as they always had done.

The hairs on her nape rose as she sensed Jasper behind her.

She blinked.

Turned.

Found him gazing down at her. Longing shone in his sparkling blue eyes.

He took her hands and raised them to his mouth, pressed gentle kisses to her fingers, her palms and then along her wrists. The sensation sparked exquisite shivers, and as she peered at his handsome face, her heart thundered in her chest, her body aching with desire.

'Is this OK?' His voice was soft, but the fire in his eyes burned bright.

'Is it OK with you?' she asked. 'Here, I mean?'

He nodded. Leant closer and slid his hand around the back of her neck, then lowered his head. He paused just inches from her lips and she took a shaky breath.

As their lips met, Ellie reached up, wrapping her arms around Jasper's neck, the scent of his cologne filling her senses as she rose on tiptoe, feeling the steady beat of his heart against hers.

Her last thought as she lost herself in him was that in his arms, she felt safe. Accepted. And loved.

26
JASPER

The next morning, Jasper woke with a start as he realised he wasn't alone in bed. He lay there for a few moments before opening his eyes. It had been so long since he'd had company overnight, other than when the children crept into his bed to seek comfort, and it was strange. He knew what had happened the night before and he knew it wasn't Kimberley next to him, but just for a second or two, he allowed himself to imagine it was. However, the thought didn't sit well with him because as much as he had loved Kimberley, and always would, he had feelings for Ellie. His heart embraced Ellie; he couldn't imagine life without her now.

Last night, they had kissed and cuddled, talked and made love. Like waking from a long slumber, Jasper was in awe of how wonderful it was being in someone's arms again. For so long he had felt numb, but now he felt alive and it was all down to Ellie and how he felt when he was with her. Yes, he had been healing slowly for some time but then Ellie had arrived in the village and everything had changed.

Opening his eyes, he turned and gazed at her. With her dark hair tumbling over the pillow, she was truly beautiful. The morning sunshine had created a shadowy light in the bedroom because, while the blinds were closed, he'd left the curtains open last night. He lay there looking at her, admiring the curve of her neck, the gentle fluttering of her dark eyelashes upon her cheeks and marvelling at how much he cared for her already.

Not wanting to disturb her, he slid out of bed and grabbed his shorts and T-shirt and left the bedroom, planning on making coffee and breakfast. He dressed in the family bathroom, then headed downstairs to let Wiggy out.

The dog wagged his tail, then scampered outside to go for a wee before sitting on the doorstep and watching some seagulls soaring over the sea. Wiggy loved watching birds and would sit there for hours, occasionally letting out a bark of excitement.

He made a pot of coffee, then some pancake batter and heated the pan. He poured batter into the hot frying pan, then added some organic blueberries. The fresh morning air entered the kitchen and Wiggy came with it, nose raised as he sniffed at the pancakes.

'Don't worry, boy, I'll keep one for you,' Jasper said with a smile and the dog gave a soft woof of appreciation. 'I don't know if you noticed, but we had company overnight.'

Wiggy tilted his head as if considering what Jasper had said.

He turned the pancakes over, before grabbing some mugs and a tray from the cupboard. He added a small jug of milk, sugar, and some cutlery, then placed the cooked pancakes onto a plate. After he'd chopped one pancake up, he dropped it into Wiggy's bowl.

'Enjoy.'

He closed the bifold doors, carried the tray upstairs and went into the bedroom. He set it down on the bedside table and got into bed.

'Good morning,' he said as Ellie stirred.

'Morning.' She smiled sleepily up at him. 'What time is it?'

'Just after nine.'

'Nine?' She sat up and the covers dropped, so she grabbed them and covered herself shyly. 'How did we sleep so long?'

'We had a busy night.' He laughed and heat filled his cheeks. It had been a busy night, and he had enjoyed every minute of getting to know Ellie better. 'I guess we needed the rest.'

She pushed a hand through her dark hair. 'I guess we did.'

'Coffee?'

'Please.'

Her smile dropped. 'Oh god! Gran will wonder where I am.'

'You sent her a message last night. Remember?'

She frowned, then nodded slowly. 'I did, didn't I? It slipped my mind. But then, as you said … we were busy.' Her smile made his chest tighten. She was so beautiful.

'Here.' He handed her a mug of coffee. 'What exactly did you say to your gran?'

'Just that I was with you and she shouldn't worry.' Ellie brushed a finger over her bottom lip and Jasper wanted to move closer and kiss her the way he'd done last night. 'Oh man, she's going to tease me about this.'

'Why?' Concern filled him. Would Pearl disapprove?

'Well … She knows I like you and has told me to relax and take things as they come, but even so… It's obvious what happened last night.' She gestured between them and Jasper laughed.

'We're consenting adults. The children aren't here. It's all good.'

He couldn't resist her any longer. He touched her cheek, then pushed her hair over her right shoulder and kissed the soft skin there. She was warm and smelt so good he wanted to keep kissing her but he knew where that would lead so he sat back and reached for his coffee instead. It was still early so they didn't need to rush a thing.

Sipping the coffee, he felt the caffeine infuse him with energy. 'I made you pancakes.'

He set his mug down, then got the plate and placed it on her lap.

'Wow!' She smiled. 'Thank you. I can't remember the last time I had breakfast in bed.'

'You should always be treated to breakfast in bed.' He handed her a fork. 'I would make breakfast for you, although on a normal day you'd have two children and a dog trying to share it.'

Ellie giggled, and relief coursed through him. That image could have put her off, but she didn't seem to mind.

'A breakfast pile on?' she asked, cutting into a pancake and offering him the fork. He opened his mouth and took the pancake, then she cut herself a piece and tasted it. 'Yum!'

'I make good pancakes.' He smiled as she offered him more.

They ate the pancakes and drank their coffee, side by side in his bed. Jasper relished the breakfast, his appetite roused by their nocturnal activities and by the welcome company. He had tried not to dwell on waking alone for the past three years, but it wasn't something he had enjoyed and not something he'd have done by choice. However, he also knew that this could be a one off as far as Ellie was concerned, or at least that it couldn't happen when the children were home. Not for a while, anyway. If something came of this between him and Ellie, then he would have to introduce the idea to his children slowly. They would always come first.

After they'd finished, Jasper placed their empty mugs on the plate on the tray, then turned back to Ellie. 'How are you?'

'I'm good. You?'

'Good.' He nodded. 'Well, better than good but … like I said last night, I don't do this and so it's taking me a bit of adjusting.'

'Me too.' She reached for his hand and held it between both of hers. 'But that's OK. We have to start somewhere, right?'

'We do. Or we'd be stuck in limbo forever.' Ellie shuffled closer to him and rested her head on his shoulder, and he kissed her hair. 'I guess I was worried that this wouldn't feel right when I woke up this morning. No other woman has ever slept in this room. The bed is new because I bought it last year but … Well, what I'm trying to say is that—'

'It's OK.' Ellie turned and placed her hands on his shoulders. 'You don't need to explain anything to me. I understand what a big deal this is, and it means the world that I'm here with you.' She kissed him gently and ran her hands up and down his arms, stroked his shoulders, neck, and face, kissing him all the time. It felt right and Jasper relaxed into her kisses, into her touch and lost himself in her.

Later, as they lay in each other's arms, Jasper stroked Ellie's hair and let himself be right there in the moment. He'd spent so many days and nights lost in grief and sadness, wishing things were different and that life hadn't been so cruel to him and his children. But with time, he'd come to accept that there were things beyond his control and all he could do was make the most of what he did have rather than regret what he didn't.

Right here and now, he had Ellie's company, and he was grateful for that.

When they'd both showered and dressed, Jasper made more coffee and was sitting at the kitchen island waiting for Ellie. Wiggy was back on seagull duty and Jasper watched him, fascinated by the dog's concentration. When he set his mind on something, he had incredible focus.

He heard footsteps on the stairs, then Ellie entered the kitchen and even though it was only minutes since he'd seen her, his stomach flipped. But then he saw her expression…

'Ellie, what is it?'

'I just … picked up my phone to check I had no messages and spotted an email. I opened it and … It was my agent.'

'Your agent?'

She nodded. 'Ramona. Well, she's not my agent now, but she was and then she dumped me. But now she says she needs to speak to me because she has exciting news.'

Ellie didn't look excited at the prospect of speaking to this Ramona. She had one arm wrapped around her waist and she was worrying her bottom lip. But surely exciting meant exciting so…

'Why don't you call her?' he asked. 'Then you'll know what it is.'

'I … I guess I could. No harm in speaking to her, is there?'

'None at all.' Jasper got off his stool and took Ellie's mug over to her. 'Here, have your coffee and I'll take Wiggy for a walk so you can have some privacy.'

'There's no need for that. I can speak to her in the lounge if that's OK?'

'As long as you're sure?'

Ellie nodded, then went through to the lounge and Jasper went to the bifold doors and perched next to Wiggy. 'Hey boy. It's a beautiful day.'

Wiggy's tail thumped against the decking and he looked up at Jasper with eyes filled with love. Jasper ran his right hand over Wiggy's head and ears, then down his back, the fur soft and warm to the touch.

It felt like hours as he waited for Ellie but soon enough; she returned to the kitchen so Jasper went to her. 'You OK?'

She nodded. 'Yes. Well, I think so. See, the things is … Ramona apologised for letting me go and said it was an oversight on her part and she did it in the heat of the moment. She said that she does value me and wants me as her client.'

Ellie sucked in a shaky breath. 'She has a role for me. Well, an audition for a role.'

'She does? Well, that's brilliant, right?' Jasper smiled.

'I think it is. But … If I secure it, it will involve some travelling and see… it's a small part in a TV show set in Iceland. It would be a start though, she said. Apparently, the director saw me audition for something else and liked me and when the actor they'd chosen for the role dropped out, he contacted Ramona and asked if I would audition for it. I mean … I know these things happen like this sometimes but it's never happened to me before and so I didn't expect it but … now it has.' She set her mug on the island and then her phone. 'But it would mean going to London for the audition and then to Iceland for five months.'

Jasper swallowed his dismay and forced his lips into a smile. Five months was a long time. Five months could change everything. But … if this was what Ellie wanted, then he would never stand in the way.

'Ellie, this sounds like a brilliant opportunity.'

'It does. I know that.'

'If it's what you want, then you have to go for it.'

She wrapped her arms around herself. 'But this … us. Where would that leave us?'

Her eyes searched his face, and he sighed inwardly. What could he say to make this right for her?

'We'll find a way if this is meant to be.'

He opened his arms, and she stepped into his embrace. He held her tight, wishing his heart would slow down. Wishing things could be simple for once. Wanting Ellie to do what was right for her because he would never want to deter her from chasing her dreams. But he couldn't help wondering what it would mean for them when this was all so new. Wondering if their dreams were destined to intertwine, or if they were like ships drifting on different currents, never meant to dock at the same shore.

27
ELLIE

After leaving Jasper's, Ellie went to the beach. She needed time to untangle the knot of emotions Ramona's words had created, each syllable replaying in her head. A few weeks ago, she'd have said it was exactly what she wanted, but now she wasn't so sure. Yes, it was an opportunity, but was it the right one for her? Spending the night with Jasper, being with him in his home and enjoying the way he treated her had opened her eyes to how things could be with the right man.

But what she needed to be certain of was if Jasper was the *right* man for her. After all, he had two young children who could also be hurt if the relationship failed. Plus, there was Jasper's grief for his wife that meant he was vulnerable and Ellie would never want to hurt him or cause him more pain. He'd been through quite enough for one lifetime.

'What to do, Ellie, what to do?' she muttered to herself as she strode along the sand, her sore ankle twinging slightly at the brisk pace.

How did you know when something was right? How could she choose between Jasper and her acting career? Until today, she'd been all but certain that it was over, anyway. She'd turned her back on the life she'd had in London, ready to embrace a life in Cornwall, but now that old life had reared its head again and was tempting her back. There was no guarantee she'd get the role, and it was also a small role; it could be a road to nowhere. But so could her relationship with Jasper. It depended what she wanted. What she saw her future being like.

'But what do I want?' She tucked her hands into her pockets and upped her pace.

With the sky turning grey, a brisk, cooler breeze whipped at her hair and clothing. The morning had started out fine, but now it looked like they could have a storm. The breakers frothed as they hit the shore, curling inwards like they would swallow the sand in one giant gulp. Saltwater spray flew up into the air, then scattered like diamond drops that landed on the sand.

As the tide lapped at her toes, Ellie stepped backwards. The last thing she needed right now was to have cold, wet feet. That wouldn't help her focus at all.

Why did this have to happen? Was it life's way of testing her commitment to Cornwall and to Jasper? She'd enjoyed being home, spending time with her gran and with Jasper and his children. Had felt content for the first time in years. No one was judging her, no one was telling her she was less than she was. And yet ... the glamour of her London life had been one thing that had kept her there. Imagine what Barnaby would say if she secured a big role. His parents too. Their actions had made her feel insignificant, and it hurt; but then, she came home to love and acceptance. She had, at last, felt safe.

But this role could be the start of something incredible. The break she'd been waiting for…

As thunder cracked the sky, she shivered. It was time to head home and make some big decisions. Having one thing didn't have to mean sacrificing the other, but she also knew that she couldn't have it all. People's hearts were at stake, hers included, and so she wouldn't hurry this decision, even though Ramona had told her she needed to know ASAP.

With the sky breaking open and rain lashing down, Ellie ran up the beach towards her gran's, each footfall sending up a spray of sand and seawater.

What was it people sometimes said? You only regret the chances you don't take? Perhaps it was time for Ellie to take a chance. Perhaps it was time for her to put herself first.

Perhaps she should follow her heart…

28
JASPER

The children were due home in an hour and Jasper had already cleaned the house from top to bottom, baked some peanut butter cookies and walked Wiggy twice. He had emptied the washing basket and ironed all the dry clothes. If he'd been able to focus, he'd have done some work too, but his mind was too chaotic to concentrate and so physical activity had been the order of the day for him.

He went to the bifold doors and opened them, then stepped out onto the decking. The air rushed over him, refreshing and salty, laced with the sweet fragrance of the spring flowers growing in his garden. He had planted wild flower seeds in the borders with the children and they were flowering now, a plethora of colours to encourage bees and butterflies to visit. After the storm that had rolled in the previous day, everything seemed cleansed and renewed. Sometimes a good storm was necessary to clear the air.

He hadn't seen or heard from Ellie since yesterday when she'd left his home. They'd had one amazing night together, then she left, leaving Jasper wondering what would happen next. He had encouraged her to think of herself and what she wanted from her future. As much as he'd have liked for her to say that she wanted to be with him and his children, it was too soon for her to make such a momentous decision. Besides which, the last thing he wanted was to put pressure on her. If she decided not to audition, then regretted it, she could end up resenting him and the children and that would be a horrid situation to be in. But letting her go hadn't been easy, and now he felt raw. Raw with sadness. Raw with confusion. Raw because for the first time since he'd lost Kimberley, he had opened his heart to another. He had, perhaps against his better judgement, let Ellie in, and now he was a wreck. Was it worth it then, allowing another human being to get close? Since he'd lost his wife, he'd shut himself down to all emotional connections except to his children, but Ellie had got to him and he'd thought it was worth taking a chance.

Wiggy nudged his leg with his nose and Jasper reached down and patted him. 'Good boy,' he said. 'If only everything in life was as simple as a dog's love and devotion.' In response, Wiggy wagged his tail, then sat down next to Jasper to keep him company.

He suspected Ellie would go to London for the audition and get it. How could she not? She was incredible and he could picture her on TV, her beautiful face, her sweet voice, and that glow she had about her. On the big screen, she would attract thousands of admirers and secure future roles, and then she'd move to Hollywood and…

Shaking his head, he laughed. He was getting carried away, and it was ridiculous. Yes, that could all happen, but if it did, he wished Ellie well. Being with her, even just for one night, and getting to know her over the past two months had helped him. There was no denying the positive impact she'd had on him and his children, and he would always be grateful for that. Even if she left now and nothing came of the connection they had, he would be grateful for the time with her. Ellie had, in a short time, taught Jasper that he could feel again, he could enjoy the sunshine on his face and the breeze on his skin, he could savour the flavours of food and sleeping in late for the first time in years. He had no doubt that he wouldn't get close to anyone else because Ellie was special and that was why she had got to him, but just being able to care about another woman had helped a part of him to heal. Ellie had aided his recovery from the depths of despair that he'd once thought he'd never escape.

There was a life to be lived and while he wished Ellie could be part of that life, he could still enjoy the time he had left. He could still be the best father possible and the best dog dad. The embers of what he'd shared with Ellie would keep him going as she had restored the warmth to his heart and life.

Hearing a car pull up, he went to the front door. It was time to welcome his children home.

29

JASPER

A week passed, and Jasper hadn't heard from Ellie. The children were back at school and there were signs of early summer everywhere he looked. Not wanting to put pressure on Ellie, he'd refrained from contacting her and had stayed away from The Garden Café, too. With the children at school, it was easier because they weren't there asking him to go for breakfast or questioning why he didn't want to go.

Initially, he'd felt quite stoic about what had happened, but with each day that passed, his heart had begun to ache. It was a low, dull ache that nagged at him like a sore muscle or a sensitive tooth. He knew why. Reality was setting in. The reality that Ellie would leave the village and he'd never see her again or only on the TV screen. The reality that he'd found someone, a woman who could be his person, and then he'd lost her. And not just him, but his children. They had asked after Ellie, wondered where she was and why they hadn't seen her, and that had made him curse himself for letting her in. After all, if he hadn't allowed her to spend time with them, then none of them would have become fond of her. None of them would have known her to miss her. It was all his fault.

After dropping the children at school, he walked to the café. He wasn't sure why because he didn't want to go there, but it was like he couldn't help himself. Even if it was just to say goodbye, then that was better than nothing. If she wasn't already gone, that was, because he knew she could have left by now. But something drew him there, and he realised he needed to try to see her one last time, however painful that would be. It was time for some closure.

At the café gardens, he let himself through the gate and walked inside.

And there she was. Bag on her shoulder. Suitcase at her side. Saying goodbye to Pearl.

His heart squeezed then, fit to break.

Turning, he grabbed the gate and yanked it open, wanting to get away before she spotted him. It turned out he wasn't brave enough to say goodbye after all.

30

ELLIE

'Are you sure about this now?' her gran asked after she'd released her from their hug. They'd come to the café that morning to have breakfast and for Ellie to see the chickens before she left for London. She'd grown fond of the birds and didn't like to leave without seeing them.

Ellie gave a one shoulder shrug. Chewed at a ragged cuticle. Placed a cool hand on her forehead and sighed.

'I just don't know, Gran. But I'm worried because if I don't take this chance, then will I always wonder?'

'It's possible, but what about everything else? You could end up wondering about that too.'

Ellie sighed. She knew her gran was right. She'd thought about nothing else for the past week. She hadn't heard from Jasper and had taken that as a sign that perhaps it wouldn't work between them after all. Or, she had seized on the fact that he hadn't contacted her as a sign because she'd wanted to be free from guilt as she made this huge decision. Ellie could easily have contacted Jasper, but pride and fear of what he might say had prevented her from doing so and now she was left wondering if she'd done the right thing. They hadn't spoken about things since she'd left his home after they'd spent the night together. The thought that he could be hurting was awful, and yet she'd done nothing to assuage that feeling. Taken no positive action to put things right. Like a petulant child, she was trying to ignore the right course of action because it was hard to face, and she knew she was in the wrong.

The gate of the gardens slammed shut, and she saw a flash of blue as someone disappeared behind the hedge. She looked back at her gran and asked, 'Who was that?'

Her gran raised her brows. 'Who do you think?'

'Oh god! What am I going to do?'

'Only you can decide that, sweetheart. This is your choice to make.'

'I don't have to choose one thing though, do I? I could still go for the audition *and* be with Jasper.'

'You should discuss that with him. As long as acting is still what you want to do. I remember what you said about it when you came home to the village and how you were feeling about it then. Search your heart, Ellie, and make sure that it is what you want because it's a hard career. You know that. You also know it could be a wonderful career for you. And if that's what you want, then go for it. But as for Jasper, you'll only know how he feels if you speak to him.'

Ellie wavered as she recalled all the times she'd felt *less than*. Less pretty. Less talented. Less relevant. Less than a human being should ever feel. She hoped it wasn't that way for every actor, but for her, the dream job she'd aspired to have had not been what she'd dreamt of. Her gran was right. Coming back to Cornwall had helped to heal something inside her she'd thought she'd lost. Her sense of who Ellie Cordwell was, who she aspired to be, and how she mattered to those who loved her. In London, she hadn't mattered to anyone, but now, for Ramona, there was a chance to make some money. She hadn't cared for Ellie before and had humiliated her when she was at her lowest ebb. The same applied to Barnaby and his parents. There had been no one who cared about Ellie there, no one who loved her the way she was loved here.

Ellie belonged in Cornwall. It was where she felt happy. Where she felt safe. Where she belonged.

'Oh, Gran!' She dropped her bag next to the case. 'Can you cancel the taxi?'

Her gran smiled. 'Are you sure?'

'More certain than I've ever been about anything. This is where I want to be. It's my home.'

She hugged her gran, then ran to the gate.

'Go tell him, Ellie!' Her gran blew her a kiss.

'I will!' Ellie opened the gate and dashed through.

31

JASPER

So she was leaving the village and Jasper behind. He walked briskly, his eyes moist and his throat tight. He'd been stupid to hope that she might not go, but then he was a fool. A stupid, hopeful fool who needed to take a reality check and forget about love. Jasper had loved and been loved once and that should be enough for a lifetime. He simply wasn't meant to fall in love again and so he'd—

'Jasper!'

He froze. Stared out over the beach below without seeing a thing. *What was that?*

'Jasper, please wait!'

Ellie. She was calling him. Or was it his stupid imagination fooling him again?

Too afraid to turn around, he stood there with his hands in his jean pockets, gazing out at the scenery. To focus on what was in front of him, he screwed up his eyes and then rubbed them before opening them again. The sunlight twinkled on the surface of the sea making it look like it was filled with sparkling diamonds. The sand was golden and speckled with shells and driftwood, dried seaweed and small pieces of sea-glass polished by the waves.

'Jasper!'

It was her.

Footsteps pounded the path, echoing the beat of his aching heart.

He closed his eyes. Took a deep breath.

She probably wanted to say goodbye.

'Jasper. Hey … Thanks for waiting.'

He turned and looked at her, and his chest squeezed. Every time he saw her, she was more beautiful than he remembered.

'Ellie,' he said, incapable of formulating any other words.

'Jasper …' She was breathing hard from running. 'I'm sorry I… haven't been in touch. I thought y-you'd need some time. And … I-I needed some time too.'

'I understand.' He pressed his lips together. His heart was beating so hard he felt like it would burst out of his chest. The world around him seemed distant, muffled. His palms were clammy, his fingertips tingling with the weight of anticipation. Every second he waited for her to speak felt like an eternity. His thoughts darted from hope to dread, chasing each other in frantic circles like a puppy might chase its tail.

'Being an actor was what I wanted for so long and I put everything I had into it.' Her dark hair was in a messy bun, but some strands danced around her face in the breeze. Her knee-length black dress clung to her curves, reminding him of the night they'd spent together. The night he'd opened his heart to her. 'But it didn't make me happy.'

He scanned her face, trying to work out what she was telling him.

'Being here in Cornwall with my gran at the café makes me happy. Baking and creating new dishes makes me happy. You, Jasper. You and the children and Wiggy, you make me happy. Ramona's message surprised me, and I admit I wondered for a while if I really wanted it. The last thing I'd ever want would be to have regrets. I owed it to myself and to you to think it through properly. I even got as far as booking a taxi to take me to the station today but do you know what?' Her green eyes roamed his face, clear as emeralds, glistening with emotion.

Jasper shook his head. His thoughts were muddled. His heart was aching.

'I knew deep down that I wasn't going to go. It was like I had to push myself to check it wasn't what I wanted, like I was auditioning myself for a role I no longer wanted to play. I don't want to be the struggling actor anymore. I don't want to be uptight, lonely and degraded, longing to be noticed. I want to be Ellie Cordwell. I want to stay here and help Gran make the café even better. I want to take some courses and learn how to prepare delicious food. Hell, I even want to run cooking courses at the café and help others to make good meals on a budget, to teach and bake and walk on the beach and swim in the sea. I want to do all of this but I also want to ask you to give me a chance to prove myself to you.'

A tear rolled down her cheek and plopped onto her dress. It sat there on the material like a flawless diamond and Jasper couldn't help himself. He touched a finger to it, then curled his hand around it.

'You don't need to prove anything to me, Ellie. This isn't another audition. If you want me, us, you've already got the part.'

'What?' she asked, more tears flowed from her eyes now, dampening her cheeks.

'The part in our lives. It's yours if you want it.' Jasper held out his hand and Ellie took it and her tear was pressed between their palms, sealing the deal.

'Jasper… I thought I'd left it too late.'

'It's never too late, Ellie, where love is concerned.'

He stepped forwards and cupped her face then he leant over and kissed her. She wrapped her arms around his waist and their kiss deepened.

In a nearby hedge, a blackbird warbled, rich and melodic, the rising and falling notes of its song like a soothing lullaby. On the beach, waves lapped gently at the shore. And from along the path, there came the sound of applause as Pearl Draper clapped her hands.

When they finally came up for air, Jasper gazed into Ellie's eyes and he saw his future within them. 'I love you, Ellie.'

'I love you too, Jasper.'

They kissed again and then she said, 'Do you fancy getting a coffee?'

'Where?' He frowned as if confused but laughter bubbled in his chest.

'How about at The Garden Café?' She giggled.

'Sounds good to me.'

Holding hands, they retraced their steps to the café. The world felt brighter now, as though the weight that had pressed on his chest was finally beginning to lift. The warmth of Ellie's hand in his grounded him, steadying him in a way he had craved for a long, long time.

When they reached the café, for the first time in a long while, Jasper could breathe freely. His healing journey wasn't over, but with Ellie by his side, he felt ready for whatever came next. He knew they would face it together.

EPILOGUE - ELLIE

Four weeks had passed since Ellie had made the decision to stay in Porthpenny. The day she'd been packed and ready to leave still lingered in her mind, and she'd thought a lot about what had happened before and after that. She suspected she had simply been testing herself to see if leaving and returning to London was what she wanted. The audition had, of course, been an amazing opportunity. For someone. But not for her. Ellie was certain now that her future lay in Cornwall with Jasper, Mabel, Alfie, Wiggy and her gran.

Sitting on a blanket on the sand, Ellie watched as Jasper and the children splashed in the shallows of the sea with Wiggy joining the fun. The late May day was sunny and clear with a warm breeze. Ellie was wearing shorts and a T-shirt along with a sunhat and sunglasses. While the others played in the sea, she was making notes in her notebook about her ideas for the café. Along with her gran, she'd been planning a special summer menu and visiting local farms and small businesses to get inspiration for new dishes she could create.

Since her return to Cornwall, she had rediscovered her love of cooking and enjoyed the serenity it brought her. Acting had never done that. In fact, it had made her tense and anxious, as tightly coiled as a steel spring. She had thought her life lay in that direction and initially been devastated when she'd been dumped first by her agent and then by Barnaby, but now she knew it was the best thing that could have happened to her. Sometimes, things had to go wrong before they could go right and as her gran had always said to her: *Everything happens for a reason. You won't always know what that reason is at the time but one day, it will all become clear.* Now, Ellie could trust in those words because she had finally reached a point in life where she felt happy and secure.

Closing her notebook, she put it down and gazed out at the sea. The sun warmed her skin, bathing the scene in a rich golden light. She removed her hat and let the breeze tousle her long hair while an easy smile played on her lips. Jasper was chasing the children around and then he grabbed Alfie and threw him over one shoulder. Alfie screamed and laughed and then Jasper chased after Mabel. She ran away as quickly as she could while Wiggy barked and jumped around them. Wiggy's fur glistened with salt water, and he bounded in and out of the waves, his tail wagging happily.

Ellie's heart swelled with love and contentment. This little family might not have been created by her, but she had inherited them when she'd fallen in love with Jasper and already loved them like they were her own. Jasper. Mabel, Alfie. Wiggy. Each of them had made their way into her heart and she would always love them and be there for them. She wouldn't always get things right, but she was learning how to be a partner, how to be a friend, how to be a mum and dog mum.

Every laugh, every splash, every bark was like a promise of more to come. She felt deeply connected to the life they were building together in a way she'd never felt to her life in London. Sometimes things were just right, and this was what she had found in Cornwall. Ellie was in love with Jasper and with the life they were living right now, but also in love with the moments that lay ahead, as yet unknown but to be filled with love and connection.

Ellie turned around to get her phone from her bag so she could take some photos. She wanted the children to be able to have a new photo album each so they could fill them with more memories. She had made two copies of the photos in the album Kimberley had created for them, so the children had one each and Jasper had one too. But she also believed it was important for them to capture the here and now, and so she was taking as many photos as possible for them.

As she stood up she heard a deep laugh.

'Hello there, beautiful lady. Thought you'd sit here and watch, did you?'

'Jasper!' She whirled around and gasped as he took her hand in his cold, wet one. Droplets of water shone on his skin and his muscular chest was tanned from his time at the beach. 'I was going to take some photos of you all.'

'Plenty of time for that,' he said, taking her phone and dropping it into her open bag. 'But for now, it's time for fun.'

'What?' Panic filled her chest, and she tried to pull away but he held her hand tight.

'You know you want to.' He winked and she giggled.

'No. It's too cold.'

'Come on, Ellie!' Alfie called as he waved at her. 'Come and paddle.'

'Oh god...' She looked down at herself then made a decision. She undid the tie holding her shorts up and pulled her T-shirt over her head.

'To the sea, my lady!' Jasper said as he scooped her into his arms then ran towards the water.

She clung to his neck, laughing hard as he splashed into the shallows then waded deeper. Cold water surrounded them, but she clung tight to him and soon they were immersed up to Jasper's elbows.

'It's freezing,' Ellie said from between clenched teeth as the sea lapped at her skin.

'You'll soon get used to it.' Jasper kissed her. 'Like everything in life, really.'

He turned them so they could watch the children as they took turns to throw Wiggy's ball. The dog chased happily after it then brought it back for another go.

'I feel incredibly lucky that I'm here and have a chance to get used to this,' Ellie said. 'Things could have been so different.'

'All we have is the here and now.' Jasper squeezed her against him, and she tightened her arms around his neck.

'I know, my sweet. Every day is a gift when I get to spend it with you.' She kissed him softly, her heart swelling with love.

Whatever the future might hold, for now there was love. So much love. So much joy. And hopefully the promise of more to come.

Ellie had returned to Cornwall a single woman who'd been rejected by those who should have cared about her. But in leaving that life behind, she had found her family and found a love to last a lifetime.

And it had all happened when she'd come to spend spring at The Cornish Garden Café…

The End

Get ready to continue this gorgeously uplifting series with ***Summer at The Cornish Garden Café!***

WANT MORE?

Visit my website here - https://rachelgriffithsauthor.com to subscribe to my newsletter, to download free short stories and find out what's next.

Like my Amazon page here https://www.amazon.co.uk/stores/author/B0716H4KXG to receive alerts about new books and deals.

Take a look at ***Also by Rachel Griffiths*** for plenty more delightfully uplifting stories!

DEAR READER,

Thank you so much for reading *Spring at The Cornish Garden Café*. I hope you enjoyed reading the story.
I would be very grateful if you'd leave a rating and a short review sharing your thoughts and feelings about the story.
Stay safe and well!
With love always,
Rachel X

ACKNOWLEDGMENTS

Firstly, thanks to my gorgeous family. I love you so much!

To my friends, for your support, advice and encouragement.

To everyone who buys, reads and reviews this book, thank you. XXX

ABOUT THE AUTHOR

Rachel Griffiths is an author, wife, mother, Earl Grey tea drinker, gin enthusiast, dog walker and fan of the afternoon nap. She loves to read, write and spend time with her family.

WANT MORE?

Visit my website here - https://rachelgriffithsauthor.com to subscribe to my newsletter, to download free short stories and find out what's next.
Like my Amazon page here https://www.amazon.co.uk/stores/author/B0716H4KXG to receive alerts about new books and deals.
Take a look at *Also by Rachel Griffiths* for plenty more delightfully uplifting stories!

ALSO BY RACHEL GRIFFITHS…

Cwtch Cove Series
Christmas at Cwtch Cove
Winter Wishes at Cwtch Cove
Mistletoe Kisses at Cwtch Cove
The Cottage at Cwtch Cove
The Café at Cwtch Cove
Cake And Confetti at Cwtch Cove
A New Arrival at Cwtch Cove

A Cwtch Cove Christmas (A collection of books 1-3)

The Cosy Cottage Café Series
Summer at The Cosy Cottage Café
Autumn at The Cosy Cottage Café
Winter at The Cosy Cottage Café
Spring at The Cosy Cottage Café
A Wedding at The Cosy Cottage Café

A Year at The Cosy Cottage Café (The Complete Series)

The Little Cornish Gift Shop Series
Christmas at The Little Cornish Gift Shop
Spring at The Little Cornish Gift Shop
Summer at The Little Cornish Gift Shop

The Little Cornish Gift Shop (The Complete Series)

Sunflower Street Series
Spring Shoots on Sunflower Street
Summer Days on Sunflower Street
Autumn Spice on Sunflower Street
Christmas Wishes on Sunflower Street
A Wedding on Sunflower Street
A New Baby on Sunflower Street

New Beginnings on Sunflower Street
Snowflakes and Christmas Cakes on Sunflower Street
The Cosy Cottage on Sunflower Street
Snowed in on Sunflower Street
Springtime Surprises on Sunflower Street
Autumn Dreams on Sunflower Street
A Christmas to Remember on Sunflower Street
Secret Santa on Sunflower Street
Starting Over on Sunflower Street
The Dog Sitter on Sunflower Street
Autumn Skies Over Sunflower Street
Christmas Magic on Sunflower Street

A Year on Sunflower Street (Sunflower Street Books 1-4)

Standalone Stories
Christmas at The Little Cottage by The Sea
The Wedding

The Cornish Garden Café Series
Spring at the Cornish Garden Café
Summer at the Cornish Garden Café
Autumn at the Cornish Garden Café
Winter at the Cornish Garden Café

Printed in Great Britain
by Amazon